Ruan's Beach Getaway
Book 2
of
Ruan's Getaway Series
Ruan Willow

Dedication

This book is dedicated to those who seize moments with their lovers, who savor their lovers, and those who mutually expand their sexuality together. May you find so much pleasure you burst!

Table of Contents:

Prologue

The waves crash against the cream-colored sand on repeat below me as my fingers massage my clitoris. The waves roar and calm as I edge, raising my desire, pushing and pulling myself, ramping up to full climax just as the water pelts the shore below on repeat. It's relentless. I smile, it's just as I am. Thrashing my fingers against my clit, I release a moan, but the crash of the sea drowns it out. The crescendo of my lust rages. The swollen peak of my orgasm groans within reach.

My phone buzzes on the little table beside me on the deck. The sun beats my skin as I reluctantly abandon my swollen pussy.

"Stopping only because I know it's you," I whisper breathlessly. I tap my phone on. "My pussy is leaking, and you need to help me."

Sebastian's immediate eruption of laughter makes me smile through my waning panting.

"That's how you answer the phone?" His chuckles continue. I can hear his smile still in his words.

"Yes, when it's you," I mutter breathlessly. "When will you arrive?" My impatience makes me sound whiny. "I need you."

"Well, shit. Wish I wasn't stuck in traffic. I thought I'd already be there by now. Best I can tell, I'm twenty minutes away, but with this slow-moving traffic, there is no way I'm making it there in twenty." He gives a disgusted guffaw. "With you sounding like that, my dick just grew to giant status."

I tease my clit. "Mmmm. Want... that... inside... my hot wet pussy... right fucking now," I mutter in broken speech between heavy puffs of breath.

"Wow! Listen to you! Really wish I was there. Fuck!" He groans. "I love it when you can't breathe like that." There is a thud.

"You okay?" I whisper. "I heard a bang."

"Yeah. Fuck! Why can't I be there? I want you so bad!" He sighs. "I just smacked the dash. All is ok. Wasn't a crash."

I snicker at his impatience. "Ha! Good. I love driving you crazy like this. Let your edging begin."

He scoffs. "Has it ever ended?" He sighs heavily, like he just came. "I think we are going to top the fucking we did at the cabin while we're on the beach. I can't fucking wait."

I giggle as I touch my labia lips. "I know, right? Though I'm not sure we can top that epic fuck fest. And. Oh. Guess I should tell you. I'm touching my lips right now. They are wet. Really wet. Puffy." The ocean breeze sweeps across my wet crotch, but it stands no chance of drying me up. I bite my lower lip, breaking my grin. My fuck-me face erupts. I take a selfie with my stiffened nipples in the pic and send it to him.

I wait for it as he jabbers on about his frustration with the traffic.

"Fuck me!" he exclaims.

I erupt with laughter. "Fucked myself with Hank in doggy in the middle of the night thinking about you."

He gasps. "Fuck fuck fuck fuck fuck!" He releases a man growl that makes my clit twitch. "You trying to kill me with my boner? All the blood in my body is now in my boner. I'm gonna crash from horniness!" He pauses. "And Hank? In doggy? Oh, fuck me! You might make me crash yet."

"Well, don't do that. I need you and your cock and your luscious mouth and your expert hands and ... fuck!" I moan as I crash over the edge and plunge fully into the vast abyss of orgasm.

"Shit!" he screams like it's murder.

Then there's a loud crash sound of metal on metal as he lets out a blood-curdling scream.

I sit up straight and gasp.

#

The cabin in the mountains had brought us to sexual bliss as we indulged each other's fantasies. It was just sex. Well, with some romance shoved in. The whole weekend read like an erotica novel, because that's what it was.

Chapter One
Ruan

I pace in front of the door, my bare feet smacking the tile on repeat as I travel back and forth. Every time I get close to the matching ginormous vases that flank the front door of the rental beach house, I swivel quickly, but not before I take note of the embracing couple embedded in the flowers on each vase's face. It's a pleasant image, but it hurts to see now.

"Goddammit, Sebastian! Call me back already!" I screech into the cool air flowing from the vent above me. The blast of coolness is not helping me cool down one bit.

As I pivot, my phone buzzes. I freeze and tap it to answer. "Sebastian! Are you okay?"

He sighs heavily. "Yes. I'm fine. The man behind me crashed into me and it shoved my car into the one in front of me. But I'm fine."

"Omigod! I was terrified when I heard that crash sound!" The fear that raced through my body at that moment, and the dread for the next, the feelings that still are lingering, is not wasted on me. Of course, I care for him, but the sick rot gut of not knowing hurt more than I would have expected.

"Where are you? Do you need me to come get you?" I chew on my lip as I shift back and forth on my hips. The ties on my bikini bottoms drag against my skin as I move. I gasp for no reason at all.

"Are you okay?" he asks, his voice full of concern.

"Yes. We are talking about you right now! I'm safe in a house and you were just in a car accident. My focus is on you!"

He chuckles. "Aw. Well, aren't you the sweet, concerned girlfriend?"

I smile at the word. Having shifted to calling each boyfriend and girlfriend had set a jewel in my gut and a permanent blush to my cheeks. I'm dating a younger man. It's official. As lovely as it is, that jewel is shrouded with a bit of guilt and a bunker load of shame I'm hiding from. Shedding even the last stain of guilt will likely never happen, but I always forget it when I'm with him, when I'm chatting with him, or FaceTiming.

"Of course, I'm scared! You could have been hurt!"

"Good to know I'm not just a walking boner to you." He laughs at his own exaggerated teasing.

"Oh well, that's not such a bad thing." I guffaw as I collapse on the plush couch, plopping my bare heels on the glass of the coffee table. I can't keep the relief out of my voice. "At least you aren't hurt." I'd have waited on him hand and foot all week had that been the case.

"No, it's not. And my boner would get to you if I had to walk there. Nothing is stopping our time together this week." I love the emphatic streak in his voice. "Oh. But, thankfully, my ride is here. I'm leaving my car at this repair shop. Might as well have it fixed while I don't actually need it for the week."

"True. Good idea. I can't wait to see you! I have the wine bottle open, snacks on the island, and my pussy is calling your name."

"Oh fuck, I can't wait to feel you in my arms. Wait, your pussy can talk?" he asks, amused. "I'm listening." He releases a heavy sigh, one that stirs my lust up. He laughs again before saying, "Okay, I'm getting in the vehicle. I'll see you soon."

"Great. I'll be waiting here for you on the couch in my bright orange bikini."

"Oh, well damn, I'm gonna dream about that on the ride. See you soon, babe."

"Bye," I whisper. I'm going to burst. I take a sip of wine to try to flatten the lump in my throat, but it won't go away. I furrow my brows.

"Don't get too invested, Ruan. This is just a fling." Admonishments never work, even I know that.

I saunter out into the sunshine again. The breeze is a light blow beneath the brilliant sun. The soothing crash of the waves helps to calm my bunched-up nerves. I lean on the railing, dangling my wine glass over the rail with my fingers. Off in the distance, a couple walks along the waterline holding hands. A rusty-colored golden retriever hops alongside them in the water, jumping back and barking at the waves that flood his legs on repeat. I smile and remind myself I still need to get a puppy. I miss George so much. He's happy with my ex, I'm sure. If his new wife hadn't had a kid for George to play with, I would have insisted on taking George. It ripped my heart out to agree to that divorce stipulation. A dog may prevent getaways like this, though, and Sebastian has slowly been filling my heart, in baby steps, as I allow him to.

I drain my glass and my thoughts in no time and head inside to refill. I must have spent more time on the deck than I realized because he's naked on the couch, full wine glass in his hand, feet up on the table, cock hard and standing in the air like a flagpole.

I squeal and run to him, readying myself to leap onto him by ditching my wine glass on the dark stone end table on the edge of the living room area.

He smiles and quickly sets his wine glass down on the coffee table so he can receive me into his arms.

I land on him with my full body weight, and he immediately envelopes me in his arms. It's better than heaven in a warm bath. The rush of emotions wets my eyes.

"Oh, my gawd, you feel amazing!" I mutter as I snuggle against his torso, chest, and neck, nuzzling myself against every speck of our touching skin. The smooth friction of our skin sliding against each other ramps up my lust to a boil. I roam my hands all over his chest and biceps. "And mmm. Look at these new muscles! I've been dying to touch them! I want you."

Our eyes meet, which prompts our mouths to collide. With the thick rod of his cock pressed to my belly, I grind my abdomen against his manhood.

He breaks our French kiss with a mouth smack. "Oh, fuck, I've missed feeling you on me," he whispers into my mouth.

We devour each other's open mouths, our tongues bathing, caressing, tasting each other.

I moan. He groans. It's like a trigger.

His hands caress me along my sides until he cups my upper thigh. He travels down my neck with multiple wet kisses. We are both panting like we just ran.

"Oh, fuck, you feel beyond amazing," I murmur as his mouth sucks my skin on its way toward my right breast. "Please," I beg with nothing in mind, but, yet wanting every speck of him at once.

He bares my breasts by shoving my bikini top cups below my bosom. "You overwhelm me," he says right before devouring my erect nipple. He sucks gently at first, but then goes deep with a suck that pulls my tit to his tonsils.

My head drops back and I moan deeply as I savor his suckling. His ability to deep throat my dense breasts floors me every time.

"Oh, dear gawd," I utter. The faint roar of the waves adds to the feeling of my body floating as his hands roughly paw as he sucks.

I tangle my hands into his hair as his hands meander to my back.

His hand braces me as he bites slightly into my breast.

I yelp, which turns swiftly into a loud moan.

Gulping my nipple down to his throat makes my groin ache, my clit twitch, and my lust gorges on his passion.

"Oh, shit," I mutter as his fingers find and twist my other nipple. All my plans for the weekend rush through my brain, edging my anticipation. He mentioned he has plans too. Our shared aim is to reach for and exploit each other's fantasies like no other lover ever has for us. Granted, I've had more time to develop a deficit than he has, making me needier than I'd like to admit.

"Mmmm," he moans as he meanders his kisses over to take a turn deep throating my other nipple. "Been fantasizing about doing this." His voice is soft yet insistent, horny and demanding, but also with a sense of carefulness. "Going to take my time tasting you."

I almost laugh because his urgency begs to differ, and I love it.

He wraps his tongue around my nipple and runs it all along my tightened areola and nipple tip. He's in such fine sucking mode, I don't even want him to move on yet.

"Mmmm, damn, you are driving me wild," I drawl out in a moan-like voice.

I caress his hair and neck, play with his ear tops and lobes. I couldn't get enough of him if I tried. I trace his cheeks as he sucks me, running my fingers along his hollowed cheeks, enjoying his puckered lips with my fingertips. The union of his mouth to my skin is such a sensuous place to touch, it's like touching a moment. One that will live on in my memory forever, but only lasts mere minutes.

He reaches for my pussy. Caresses my mound, dragging his fingers to my cleft to visit my waiting clit.

I moan out as he rides my swelling clitoris with his forefinger.

He slowly releases my nipple from his mouth. It pops out hard as can be and glistening. "I was gonna wait, but I can't," he mutters. "I'm not strong enough."

He tickles his fingers along my labia lips as I squirm in his lap, mewling and moaning.

He presses his fingers into my wet pussy. I groan out, arching my back, and then curling towards him as he works my pussy into a wet frenzy with his fingers.

"Fuck me, you are so wet," he murmurs against the top of my head.

"I need you in me, please. I can't wait," I manage to say through my panting.

He cradles me to his body and stands up in one swift movement, so effortlessly it's like he just picked up a feather, not a human being. He swivels and lays me gently on the couch.

"One taste before my dick tastes you," he says with direct eye contact that I hold.

He strips down my bikini bottoms as if they are greased. I watch as he throws them across the room.

With a giggle, I settle into the soft lush of the couch, the velour against my skin like a pussy willow. "Please do."

He spreads my vulva open and gives me three long swipes of his tongue before he flicks along my bean.

I thrash and writhe as he works his mouth into a full-bore sucking of my clit. I scream out as he increases his suck. Grabbing for his hair and ears, I maul him as he mouth-molests my pussy. He reaches up and ravages my tits.

My lust drives me up that climax hill and his continued sucking and tit-playing shoves me into an orgasm. I yell out as I tetter over the edge and fall silent as my vagina contracts multiple times, too many to count.

He moves his mouth down to suck out my cum from my opening as my body finishes twitching.

My sighs slow enough for me to mutter, "Cock."

He chuckles against my pussy and the vibration arouses me further.

"Fuck me, Sebastian, fuck me hard." I dribble out the words like I'm drunk. "I need you in me."

He covers my mouth with his and we French kiss deeply before he lines up his swollen cockhead at my slit.

"Please, please," I beg.

"It's yours, Ruan. All yours."

I just want to be his.

He penetrates my wet lips and we both groan out as if it's the first time we've ever had our genitals join. Instantly, I'm reminded how that first fuck after being separated from a lover is pure bliss. Our bodies remember, so the union is massively heightened; it's like a euphoric dream in real life.

He thrusts into me hard, like he can't control himself. He rides me, the friction perfect bliss. He pounds my clit to the point I'm reaching orgasm again.

I'm not quiet. I moan and yell, scream and groan uncontrollably. "Please, yes, like that," I plead. "I'm gonna again," I mutter as the orgasm consumes me, stealing my breath as my body stiffens, twitches, and convulses as my clit rocks contraction after contraction across my pussy. The flood of endorphins fills every speck of me. The euphoria is real.

He groans out as my pussy squeezes his cock inside me. The jerking of cock inside makes me smile in my now sleepy state. He grunts as he continues to pump his still hard cock into me.

"Give me it all," I whisper.

He continues to gently thrust into me. I savor every second and miss him in me already, even though he's still there. He collapses on me heavily. We both continue to pant, the delicious memory of that frenzied fuck saturating my brain.

"Mmmm. Fuck, that was more amazing than I imagined it would be."

He releases a big sigh. "I know, it was the same for me. I fantasized and jerked off to this every day since we were last together, and nothing tops being with you. No fantasy even comes close to being with you." I yearn to coddle the wistfulness in his voice, make him sound more gratified without the glimmer of sadness.

If I'm honest, though, the same exact thoughts already occurred to me, but I can't seem to speak about it. Maybe it's because acknowledging that means I want him every day, which I will never be allowed.

He shifts and nestles himself against me as I turn on my side so our fronts fully touch.

I shove all the nasty thoughts away. I'm not ruining this blissful moment.

"You're still hard," I murmur, tempted to reach down and stroke him again.

"Yes."

He wraps his arms around me. "Want to hold you. Hold this feeling."

His heart is thudding in his chest, his lungs pumping out, his pants against my breasts.

We say nothing, but simply lay together, listening to the waves through the sliding door to the deck that I never even bothered to close.

Chapter Two
Sebastian

This woman doesn't know what she does to me. A testament to her humility.

"That was delicious. Feeling the inside of you again. I can't even adequately explain it."

She nods against my chest and dare I notice tears in her eyes?

"It was amazing, Sebastian, you are amazing," she says as she hides her eyes from me by nuzzling against my chest.

Satisfying her sexually is my goal, but laying here with her after is the prize I cherish. When I was younger, the notion of afterglow was wasted on me. Now, with Ruan, it's almost my favorite part. I smile with chagrin at giving lust a new purpose.

"You are the amazing one. That was way better than I imagined, like I said." I squeeze her. "That's worth re-mentioning."

"No doubt," she says and follows it with a sigh. "I'm still getting aftershocks."

"Really? Geez, my cock should still be in you then."

"Go for it," she says haughtily with naughtiness dazzling in her eyes.

"Later, babe. I can't get enough of holding you in my arms." I'm turning into a sap. She does this to me. "I can't believe we are finally together, Ruan. I've been dying to cradle you."

She flinches.

I open my mouth to ask her, but close it quickly instead. "I have brought a few things for us to try. But I'm going to keep them all a secret but one."

She glances up at me and I'm thrilled to see that dreadful flinching look has left her face. "Oh? Do tell." She stares at me with her eyes piercing to my core.

"Okay. So, have you ever tried those BDSM spreaders? Like, they are a kind of restraint. It's called a bend-over bar."

A little evil grin spreads across her face. "Oh, I know about them, but I've never used one. Been curious though." Her face clouds. "My ex wasn't sexually curious, as you know."

Need a change of subject quick. "Thought you might be into it, at least the last time we talked about restraints. I'm not sure I could do it myself with being claustrophobic."

She snickers. "You aren't locked inside something silly!"

"Well, for me, I'm pretty severe with the whole claustrophobic thing. It also includes the feeling of being trapped in something." I take a deep breath, then release it. "It's like if I can't freely get out of something, I panic. Even, like, if it's an article of clothing, if I can't free myself easily and quickly at a moment's notice, I panic."

"Okay. I could understand that. I feel some of that too. But what turns me on about it is that I'd have no choice or ability to get away from your stimulation. I'd be forced to stay there and take it. There's something freeing in that." She wrinkles her cute nose. "Plus, I trust you not to hurt me."

I mask my shock. Hurt her? The thought of her even voicing this hadn't even occurred to me, it's so foreign. My thoughts are always of pleasuring her. "You know me and my love for doggy, so this is a bend-over one. It's great for standing up doggy, head down on the knees doggy, or even just to trap your legs open, but have your hands free." I grin big. "So, you can touch me."

"Mmmm. Interesting and good point, like I could touch you, or be stopped from it, which will drive me fucking crazy!"

"Yeah, I love the idea of making you helpless, and teasing and edging the fuck out of you until you come. I mean, don't get me wrong,

I want you touching me." A chuckle bursts from me. "But for a once in a while thing, I'd love to render you strapped in and helpless."

"So, I'd be your sex slave. Your fuck-prisoner." She bites her lower lip as she grins.

"Yessssss," I say with the exaggerated 's' as I nod. "And it's just Velcro, so you can easily be popped out of it should you start to panic."

"Yeah, that's good. Very good." Her eyes flicker with a new curiosity. Her gaze dances with a flirtatious sparkle. "I'm not going to panic. I think it will be hot to be your sex prisoner."

I just can't get enough of her willingness to experiment. Which is a refreshing change from women my age, at least the ones I've been with. Flashbacks of June flood my brain and I push them out. I don't need thoughts of that prude psycho ex when I'm with Ruan. Fuck no. Geez. Now we've both had ex thoughts within minutes of fucking.

"So, you snuck this gadget in your suitcase? I wonder if security thought it was a weapon."

"Oh, I bet they see all kinds of crazy stuff people travel with these days. Kink is on the rise."

"True. People are getting more and more adventurous. It's more the norm than most people realize." She purses her lips and narrows her eyes. "Much to my delight as an erotica author."

"Yeah. Definitely. Just like us. So. I've been reading. We will need a safe word. I'm thinking this is a good idea for both of us to do. The company I bought this spreader from suggests the green, yellow, and red-light schema. Green for go ahead, I'm good with what we are doing. Yellow is slow down because I'm getting uncomfortable or nearing a hard no boundary, and red means stop, the play is over. I'm maxed."

"Ah, yes. This I know about. I like a gradient." She traces my nipple and plucks at it to make it hard. "I love that you are educating yourself. Like a good boy."

"Yeah, and you only have to say one word to convey what you need and want with that stoplight plan." Her comment feels like a snub but I let it go because I don't really care. I'm with her and that's all I care about.

"You don't have to tell me. I study this stuff." She presses her hips to my gut, trapping my still hard boner between us. "Bend-over bar. That actually would be a good name for a real bar. I'd love to go with you."

"A damn good name for anything." I pause as my hunger balloons. "Hey. I'm starving. You mentioned food on the phone?" My stomach growls fiercely.

"Yeah, let's go have a snack. I'm starving too. And I'd love another glass of wine."

I peel myself from her, but I want to be right back to skin to skin, so I pull her to me for a hug. "Naked hugs are the best."

"Yeah, and they don't ever end as a hug."

We kiss deeply, our hands roaming each other.

"Fuck," I murmur into her open mouth. "I'm gonna wind up fucking you again." I take a step back. "Not that that's a bad thing," I smile hugely at her. "But let's slow down a bit."

She nods and grabs my hand, pulls me toward the kitchen. "I snuck a not-so-little something in my suitcase too."

"Oh," I say with a raised eyebrow. "Did you now? Do tell. I'm dying to know."

"It's a portable sex swing. It's like a mini hammock and works for comfortably supporting a tummy ride or back. When I saw this place advertised having three ceiling-mounted eye bolts, I knew exactly what it was for, so I started researching sex swings."

My dick lurches. "Fuck me! No shit?" The sex gods have heavily gifted me with this woman. But now to convince her I want all of her. Long term.

"No shit. I found the perfect one online. Many are made of heavy-duty leather, but this one is like a hammock material, so it's more lightweight. Plus, it fit perfectly inside my suitcase." She shakes her cute butt at me as she opens the fridge.

"Oh, that's cold!" she exclaims and twists away from the fridge, the cool air nicely perking up her nipples to little thimbles. "You can swing fuck me doggy or missionary, gripping my thighs or ass."

"I love gripping your thighs and ass. And you know how I feel about doggy." I pour myself a glass of wine, remembering too late my first one is still on the coffee table. I shrug and shove two of the mini sausage and cheese rolls in my mouth. "A sex swing. Fuck, this is going to be epic!"

"I know, right? And all the angles possible. It's going to blow our minds from what I've read from other reviews. And, oh, how I know how you feel about doggy alright. So does my pussy." She bends over and digs in the fridge.

"Speaking of doggy," I mutter as my cock hardens further. "I wanna fuck you right into that fridge!"

She's so distracted reading a dressing bottle that she doesn't even respond.

"This week will be about doggy, restraints, and plenty of beach fucking." I pop two more sausage thingies in my mouth. "And my secrets."

She looks up with amusement in her eyes. "Secrets?"

"Yup. For me to know, and for you to find out."

"Well, beach fucking is an absolute must."

"Get a little, or a lot, of sand in your crack." I chuckle as she screws her face into a silly expression.

"Ass crack sand does not sound like fun."

"I'll bathe you to get all the grains out. Or fuck you ragged doggy in the shower, gyrate your ass in the shower stream on repeat."

She cracks up. "You feeling a bit aggressive, Sebastian? All this doggy talk!"

"Afraid so. It's taking all my restraint right now not to come over there and bend you over that counter and go to town, babe."

"Sustenance, then fucking." She ticks her finger in the air like she's marking an imaginary tally.

"Fucking is sustenance!" I protest.

"True, very true." She slithers her arm around me from behind. "Hey, after our snack. I'm feeling romantic. Want to take a walk along the beach in our swimsuits and then take a dip in the ocean? I want to feel your wet skin on mine."

"Oh, I'm in." I shove three pieces of pineapple in my mouth. "Mm. Juicy."

"I'm gonna freshen up and put on my black bikini." She snags a few pineapple chunks and pops them into her mouth.

"I'd rather you stay naked," I say with pineapple shreds still in my mouth. I quickly swallow them so no more fly out as I talk.

"Mmmm. Well, I don't want us to get arrested, so let's save that for when we are here."

"Naked deck fucking sounds like a good plan for when we get back. Do we have neighbors to worry about?" I watch her sweet ass as she walks away. "Or maybe we want them to see." I give her backside my best fuck me eyes.

She whips around and catches the expression on my face. She cracks up. "Do I need to worry about you tackle-fucking me?"

"Yes!" I exclaim. I've got half of a mind to scoop her up and slap the bend-over spreader on her wrists and ankles and fuck her silly. "You need about 30 orgasms as prep for a beach walk, you know."

She laughs harder. "We'll never get out at this rate." She runs into the bedroom and slams the door.

"Oh, I'll get you, Ruan. No door is going to stop me!" I finish off the plate of sausage appetizers and slide off the chair. My boner swings as I walk to my suitcase. I call out, "Oh Ruan, my dick isn't going to fit nicely in my swim trunks. I'm thinking I need you to drain him, so he fits nice and snug in my swimsuit."

I lay my suitcase flat on the ground and dig around for my suit. I stand up and hang it on my dick, put my hands on my hips.

The bedroom door flings open.

"See!" I say. "It's too big. It won't fit. I need your help." I cackle heartily. My flirty beg might just get me a blow job.

She practically folds in half with laughter, which makes her beautiful breasts flop together in a generous line of delicious cleavage. "Oh, my Gawd, you are right!"

To my utter delight, she gets down on all fours and crawls to me, her pendulous breasts swinging, her hips tick-tocking back and forth. Her crawling like this could wake a dead cock. Her gaze is everything of my fantasies of every older woman I've ever jerked off to.

Once she reaches me, she plucks the suit off my cock and tosses it behind her with a snicker.

"Later," she calls after the discarded garment. She runs her hands up my shins and thighs while dragging her tongue from my knees, up my thighs to my balls. She takes each of my balls in her mouth, one at a time, and sucks them while fondling my ass cheeks. I groan as she flicks her tongue along the base of my cock. She runs her tongue up the underside of my cock and flattens it along my frenulum, where she undulates her tongue like a belly dancer moves.

"Oh, fuck," I whisper. "Oh, fuck yes, Ruan."

She stands up and grabs my cock and pulls me to the living room by it, glancing at me every other step. Her bikini bottoms are diagonal across her ass cheeks, which displays her round rump to perfection.

"Hot swimsuit. You look scrumptious in it," I say breathlessly. That's an understatement.

"Thank you." She looks me directly in the eyes and pushes my chest back with her palm, so that I fall back on the couch.

She kneels in front of me while keeping eye contact, with that sexy as fuck look on her face. "You are in need of help getting dressed, I see."

I lay back on the couch with a sigh. What a treat. Ruan sucking my cock in a beach house. Is there anything better? Well, maybe me fucking her raw doggy until she reaches forty-plus orgasms, but hey, I'm not turning down her mouth on my cock any time of day.

She nestles up between my thighs, takes my cock shaft in her hand, and licks my cock head like an ice cream cone with four straight-up slurps. She maintains eye contact as she takes the swollen head of me in her mouth. Her lips seal perfectly as she rides my cock with her mouth while stroking my shaft at the same time.

I reach over and give her some spanks. I say sternly, "Do a good job or I'll give you a spanking, mommy."

She chuckles with my cock in her mouth. The vibrations drive me wild, and I squirm beneath her.

"I know, you are probably thinking you want that." Flashbacks of the cabin flood my brain. My lust had gotten the best of me there when I went all ape shit beating her butt, not that she'd ever have admitted it, but I'm not getting that out of control this time. It was something we both had liked, but I'm not so sure we need to go that far again.

She wiggles her ass and I give it a few more taps. She moans, then shudders.

I grin. I hit a clit nerve. So, I smack her ass a little harder.

"You like those vibrations through your clit, mommy?" I hit her butt again. "I can arrange that."

She pops her mouth off my dick with a loud smack. "You going to make me do the walk of shame along the beach front with a spanked red ass, are you?" Her eyes dance with mischief as she re-consumes my cock into her hot, warm, wet mouth.

"Oh, I know you'd like that." Maybe a few more spanks since she's into it. Can't say I hate it. I give her a few more not-so-soft taps as her mouth rides my cock.

I tense as my climax rises, give her one more slap on her right butt cheek and come hard in her mouth. My cock jerks out every drop as she continues to suck my dick.

Her eyes are closed, and she says, "Mmmm."

"Fuck, I love those vibrations when you do that," I murmur as my cock discharges all my cum into her swallow.

I sigh as she gently strokes my cock while still keeping her suction going.

I rub her back.

"Wow, babe, that was hot." I stroke her hair before glancing at her backside. Damn. I did make her skin red. I reach down and gently caress the red spot.

"Ya made me red, didn't ya?"

I nod. "My bad. I get a little too into that, mommy."

She cringes.

I startle. Shit. "Oh, I'm sorry. Are you okay?"

She shakes her head, kneels up, and puts each of her hands on my thighs. "I'm perfect." She rises, her expression now happy, and luckily clearly indicating she's already over the negative slip, whatever it was. "Now, where'd that suit get flung to? I bet I can make it fit now."

"Oh, I have no doubts. I'm empty now."

She winks and rubs her hands together.

The euphoria has rendered me immobile, so I watch her search for the suit.

She saunters around and finally finds it behind the fake tree near the full-length mirror near the front door.

"Oh, we will need to make use of that mirror this week. I'm thinking doggy right there."

She laughs exaggeratedly and flings the suit my way.

"Am I gonna get fucked in any position other than doggy this week?"

Her giggles are a delight.

"Hey, I just fucked you missionary." I sit up reluctantly, trying to shed the slump the post-orgasm has slid me into.

"Good point." She slips on a pair of mirrored sunglasses that nicely compliment her blond curls and black swimsuit, her creamy, firm skin a beautiful contrast as well.

Her breasts jiggle as she walks. This suit has some lax threads that allow for her generous body movements.

"I really really like that suit, Ruan."

"Thank you. I'm already sunscreened up. If you want some, it's on the counter by the toaster." She grabs her phone and heads out towards the deck. "I'll be out here waiting for you, little boy."

I wince. I know I call her mommy, but 'little boy'? Is she just playing off of me?

Chapter Three
Ruan

With the taste of his cum still lingering on my lips, I gingerly walk across the hot deck to locate my shoes. I'm not sure I want to wear them to walk in the sand, but I want them along in case it's too hot without them. Walking on the wet sand is my plan, though. Or even in the water.

Sebastian appears on the deck, his olive skin glistening in the sunlight. He smells like banana.

"You smell yummy enough to eat." I lick my lips.

"I think you just did that." His expression is naughty.

"I might need to do it again." I widen my eyes as I give his cock a light squeeze.

"Any time you want to suck my cock, I'm all yours."

He wraps my arms around me to pull me close.

I tuck my head under his chin, where a hint of stubble betrays that he didn't shave this morning. I inhale the banana sunscreen scent off his skin. "Yummy. I wish it tasted as good as it smells, but I'm not brave enough to find out."

He unrolls his arms from my body and grabs my hand. On the way down the deck stairs, he mentions, "I brought my wallet. Maybe we can get a cocktail or ice cream at that little seaside outdoor restaurant."

I lean back exaggeratedly. "Wow! I'm impressed! You did your research."

"That I did. I also checked out the restaurants and local shops. I'd like to buy you some lingerie for you to show off for me this week."

"Oh, that sounds fun." I show my delight with him in my happy gaze. "And here I thought you were just this go lucky kid just coming along for the ride."

He cocks his head. "I'm no stranger to planning ahead."

The sun is beating down hard and proving it's eighty-five degrees with every heated second we walk. The ocean breeze tickles my skin as I breathe in the salty air.

"I can never get enough of the scent of the ocean. It feeds me on a level nothing else does."

He grins that sexy boyish grin I adore. "Not even sex?"

"Well, nothing does it like sex." I give him a googly eyed look and stick out my tongue. "But... the ocean, it does something to my soul to be near it." I try to keep the forlorn feeling from showing on my face. "I've often thought of moving to the ocean."

"Florida! You should move here. We'd be able to date like a normal couple." He wags his head up and down like a puppy dog tail. "Please. Please. Pretty please." He puts his hands together like he's praying.

"I'm pretty damn close to committing to moving. It's just my family is all back home. I'd miss them." Yeah, he says that now, but in six months, he'll be on to a new little hottie. But I'd still have the ocean then.

"Seriously, Ruan. This would be epic!" He hops around like a toddler who just got a sucker. "Just think. You and me together every day. Fuck! I'd love it!"

I nod. "Yeah, it would be pretty epic."

"Gas is much cheaper than a plane ticket." His hopeful eyes give me too much hope. "Plus, think how much we could fuck."

I chuckle and nod. My smile lingering, I say, "I like the way you think." I swing our joined hands. "Let's talk about the restaurants you found. I literally didn't have time to look any up. What looks the most promising? I'd like to take you out to dinner tonight."

"I have money. Let me treat you."

"No, Sebastian. I'll take you." The gas comment.

He grabs my hand once more and pulls me to walk in the water. Up ahead, an older couple in swimsuits under white beach coverups and beige sun hats are walking along hand in hand. A little girl squeals and runs from behind them. A little boy bursts out next. Both kids are in bright beach colors. Their sounds are so delightful and warm my heart. Their sweet elations compliment the roar of the waves as both sounds crescendo and wane.

"We are coming up on our year anniversary." He hard swings my arm by our conjoined hands. "That's something." He shakes our fists in the air.

I nod and give him a slight smile. "Yes. You are right. We are, aren't we? I have to say, I never thought we'd make it this far."

He feigns shock. "What? I'm offended." He laughs, but I can see a thread of something less than jovial in his eyes. "What, I'm not long-term material? That hurts!" He pretends to be stabbed, clutches his chest, and feigns falling.

"You goof," I shout over the roar of the wave crash.

He rights himself with a happy look as the water floods his feet. "I'm not kidding. I am long-term material. Look. I'm still here." He pounds his chest like a dominant ape, but just once.

"True. True. You are indeed."

"Where do we go next, by the way? We need a third getaway planned before we go home. To give me hope to see you again."

I'm a little taken aback by the turn of our conversation, but I play along. "Well, I have an idea brewing. I'll share once I know more."

"Aw, come on. Give me a hint." He looks angsty and it makes me giggle.

"If you pout, I'm sucking that lip."

The seagulls chirp overhead as they soar up.

He immediately sticks out his lower lip.

I clap with glee and clobber him. He catches me and we kiss. I make a point of sucking his lower lip into my mouth hard.

"Careful. You are waking up the rod," he whispers against my partially opened mouth. "It won't fit in my suit again if you aren't careful."

He kisses me again and his cock fills the void between us. I press my body fully to his as he envelopes me.

"Too late," he mutters.

"Mmm. Fuck, you feel amazing. I can't wait to feel you inside me again."

He releases a soft man growl that plays at my clit, teasing me closer to the edge when I'm already horny again.

"I love that sound," I murmur into his neck. "Please fuck me hard when we get back to the beach house, will you?"

"Beggars get to be choosers," he mutters with a lust-filled voice. "Your desire is my command, babe."

"Aw, Sebastian, you please me like no other." I remember the older couple with grandkids and figure they must be approaching us, so I pull myself away from him.

As I turn, they are nearly passing us.

They both nod. She says, "Good afternoon." Her smile is knowing, and I rather like it.

"Good afternoon," I repeat, giving her a knowing look back.

"Howdy," Sebastian says.

"Nice day," the older gentleman says.

The kids chase each other into and out of the sea as they squeal and laugh like the bright balls of energy they are. I smile at them, as does Sebastian.

As they leave, I say, "They are cute."

"Yep, kids love the water." Sebastian doesn't look as skeptical as I expected.

"Oh, I meant the couple," I tease.

"Bah!" he shouts with a wave of his arm in my direction.

I crack up. "Okay, I meant the kids. But the older couple, they were cute too."

We walk along the ocean holding hands, soaking up the ethereal crashing water sounds and the warm sun. Never ever can get enough. A day like this makes me want to move here even more.

At the restaurant, we get seated at a table on the patio facing the ocean. We pull our chairs close together on the backside of the round table so we can be as close as possible, and both still see the water. This is the first time we've gone out in public together. I glance around to assess who is looking at us. No one is eyeing us up. What do they all think? Geez. I normally don't give a shit. I shake my head to clear these odd old feelings I had shelved once I hit my forties. I'm annoyed they are creeping back.

"Looking for something? The waitress?" He's so innocent, untarred by time and ridicule.

I blow out a puff of air. "Yeah, I'm in deep need of water. Then a cocktail sounds lovely." Need to shove myself off this cliff already.

He reaches under the table and squeezes my knee just as a waitress comes up.

Her smile is lovely, her hair like black silk caressing her tanned skin as she talks. "Hey there! I'm Tamara. I'll be your waitress for today. What can I get you two?"

"I'll have water and a glass of Sauvignon Blanc." I shift in my seat but don't unsettle his hand on my knee.

"Perfect. And you, my good man?" Her expression is flirty.

Sebastian smiles. My brain goes to watching him fuck Tamara, her hair swiftly dancing across her back to swirl in the air as he fucks her from behind, hands and feet bound in the bend-over spreader. I almost gasp at the beauty of it.

"I'll take a gin and tonic with lime please," Sebastian says with a twist of his fingers. "And a water too please."

"Perfect! I'll be back." When she spins, her hair dances like a delicate wave of smoothness.

"What's that look for? You look like you saw something hot!" Sebastian gives me a wanton look.

"Yeah, erotic writer brain on high power. She's luscious and I just imagined you fucking our sexy little waitress from behind, her hair swaying like a silky fringe."

"Wow! Well, damn. I wish I lived in your brain!"

"Oh, you are in my brain alright, just like that scene that just flashed before my brain's eyes."

He shakes his head. "You just amaze me with all you create. How do you do it all nonstop?"

I lean back and smile. "It's kind of crazy. It's like anytime I'm doing something mundane where I can't do anything else, like shower or drive, my mind drifts right to sex. Images and ideas flood my brain. Then it happens again when I write or do audio. It's more like I don't have enough time to do it all rather than I get writer's block."

"Well, that's a true storyteller if I've ever heard one." He skittles his hand up my thigh towards my pussy and does one poke at my mound before snatching his hand away. "I can't resist touching you at every moment now that we are live and in person again. Do you think we will do this again soon? I mean, like really soon?"

I shake my head. "Let's enjoy now, love. We are together and let's fuck each other's brains out. Fulfill as many fantasies as we can. Live in the moment."

He sighs heavily. "I get that, but I can't help but want more of you, even though I'm with you."

The waitress drops off our drinks and I imagine me sucking her tits from between their legs as Sebastian fucks her from the other side.

I silently chuckle as she spins away.

"What? Do tell? You are giving me a solid chubby with this story, by the way."

I laugh out loud, which causes the woman at the next table over to flinch and glance my way. "Well, I just imagined me sneaking between both of your legs as you fuck her, to suck her tits."

"Fuck!" he retorts.

The woman glares at him this time, and I smile at her and wink. She turns in a huff with a 'Fff' sound.

"I know, right? I gotta make some notes when I get home. I feel a story coming on."

"And I can't wait to read it, knowing I was the inspiration. And no one in the world will know but us."

"Exactly right." I sip my wine as my brain fleshes out the story. I need to focus on Sebastian, but it's hard to turn my writer brain off. "Okay, so tell me about work. How is it going?"

"It's going. It's not my dream job, but it's okay. I've recently been toying with the idea of finishing my degree."

"Oh, you totally should. I remember you mentioned that a few weeks ago. You going to do it?"

"Yeah, I think so. It would open me up to more options for work. I really wouldn't mind that happening. I should have never stopped to begin with, but it all got to be too much, so I just told myself it was okay to put it off for a while. But now it's been a few years and I never intended this much time to go by."

"Smart attitude to do it now. I waited too long to really dig my nails into writing. I was always busy doing other things, focusing on other careers. However, I also think that if I hadn't waited this long, I wouldn't be the writer I am. So, in that way, my putting writing on a shelf helped me relax and accept myself. And if I'm brutally honest, waiting until I accepted my sexuality has made all the difference in the world."

Chapter Four
Sebastian

As we walk along the sand, a bit saturated with alcohol, I contemplate the sculpture of her words earlier with the threat of a frown. How she seems to create me as some immature youngster, how she thinks I'm just not that serious. Well, I am serious, dammit! And I want her. I keep my eyes straight ahead on our route back.

Not gonna dwell because I'm with her and she's wonderful, and we are on the beach. I successfully shed all the bullshit. I'm focusing on her, and her alone.

We surely both look like saps, our faces blissful from the alcohol and the absolution of impending intense sex. Her grin is set in some phase of pleasure already. The silence is probably allowing her head to build her erotic story, letting it play out as a fantasy as she watches the acts further unfold. To be honest, I was ready to invite the waitress over to the beach house to do Ruan's story live. Might have to bring that up with her. But, for now, I'm enjoying the sounds, scents, and the sensations of the ocean licking my feet on repeat as we walk back to the beach house. My mind drifts to the spreader and when to pull it out. My cock starts to stiffen as I picture Ruan bent over on the beach, legs held apart, wrists bound, her holes open for me to pound. Fuck! There goes my cock.

"What's going through that beautiful, sexy, erotic brain of yours, babe?" I snag a quick glance at her and soak in her blissful expression because it feels damn good.

"Just thinking about you and dreaming about what we will do this week. And how you're the best mistake I've ever made."

I lose my smile at the end of her sentence.

"I mean, I almost didn't respond to you in the first place."

My heart drops a little more. "I know. But I'm so glad you did. Because look at all the pleasure we've given each other." I stumble over what to bring up next. Do I address her comment? Do I ignore it and hope?

"I'm glad I did too. I wouldn't trade us for anything. I'm enjoying us right now, just as we are."

My resolve thickens. I've got to prove myself when I have nothing hidden. "I want you, Ruan."

She stops and spins towards me, and wraps her arms around me, pulls my face to hers. "I want you, Sebastian." Her gaze is so lusty an explosion erupts in me.

We kiss as the waves invade our ankles, bathing our feet in salty, lukewarm water. The wet swirl of sand it carries fills in around our ankles. As the wave retreats back to the sea, it efficiently buries our feet. We both pant as our kiss deepens. My cock is fully erect and pressed snug between us.

"Mmmm. You are ready," she murmurs against my neck as I kiss her bare shoulder.

I nudge the bikini strap over an inch with my tongue. "I want to undress you with my mouth."

"Well, fuck. There's a sentence," she says with passion. "Yes, fucking please."

"Oh, fuck yeah," I gasp, mirroring her podcast catchphrase. I imagine her clit swelling and I yearn to touch it.

"Oh, fuck yeah, is right," she copies in her distinctive voice.

I separate from her and ready myself to dash off by raising my arms up. "First one to the beach house gets to pick our next sex act!" I tear down the beach, kicking up sand as I run.

"Hey! Now, that's not fair!" she calls after me. "I've got way shorter legs than you."

"And they are about to be around me, so hurry that great ass up!" I shout behind me.

Of course, I win. That's a given.

When she arrives on the deck, out of breath, which by itself is a huge turn-on, I'm sitting in the lounge chair with my feet crossed at the ankles, my hands knitted behind my head.

"What took you so long?" I tease.

"Oh, don't pretend like you didn't see me give up and walk!" she chirps between pants.

"Your breathing is already where I want it, so come here." I sit up and open my arms wide, spread my thighs, and pat the wood planks between my legs. "Set your sexy little ass right here. Facing the ocean. I want to rub you into an orgasm right here on the deck."

She gives her little approving sexy smile as she lowers herself between my legs.

Getting to see so much of her skin in the sunshine is delicious.

"Blow job last round means it's my turn to pleasure you. Not that I'm keeping score, I just want to make you come."

I nestle her body to mine, so we fit. Which is not an effort at all. I press her head to my left shoulder so my right hand will be free to stimulate her clit. I wiggle my fingers into her bikini bottoms and find her lips, which are already moist, likely from the running she just did and, more obviously, her state of arousal. I tickle my fingers along her pussy lips and swipe her juices up to her clit. I spread the wetness around her clit as she moans and writhes against me, with my hard cock sandwiched between us, taking the brunt of her gyrations, which send my lust through the roof. I grunt.

She moans.

We are charging our way up the edging to orgasm hill just like that.

I increase the speed of my fingers as I whisper above her ear, "I'm gonna make you cum hard and often, then I'm going to fuck you so much your body will be swimming in endorphins for hours." I deftly work my fingers on her genitals as rapidly as I can manage. "Gonna fuck you, Ruan. Gonna fuck you hard and long and drive you to so many orgasms, you'll never forget." I spank her clit as she lurches forward and then leans back to writhe against my body.

Her wetness increases. I use it to manipulate her clit, which sends her into a delicious frenzy of moans, groans, and whimpers that make my cock twitch against her back.

"Fuck," she coos. "Shit."

She shifts her hips back and forth as I relentlessly ride her magic bean. Her movements arouse me further as she rubs my erection.

"Oh, my gawd, Sebas..." she says, but can't finish because the orgasm steals her words.

The satisfaction for me is real as she arrives at her peak. Her upper body curls forward and her feet leave the lounge chair and levitate above it as she twitches out her climax.

"Oh, fuck yes, I love your sounds. Let it all out. Fuck, you are just amazing." I keep rubbing her clit at the same pace until I'm sure she's reached the full apex of her orgasm high. Her sighs tell me it all. "Aw yeah. Just like that. Just like that," I encourage.

She falls silent for a good thirty seconds and remains still while still significantly panting.

"Oh, damn, that was big," she says softly.

I chuckle. "Sure seemed that way." I won't lie. It strokes my ego to make her cum. I start to stimulate her clitoris again.

Within seconds, her shoulders curl forward. I love striking at her when she's already hot, it usually brings her multiple orgasms like rapid fire.

"Going," she says with a gasp. "Going again."

I keep rubbing her clit, then ramp it up even a bit faster and she screeches out, twists her head to the side against my chest, and then she goes silent as her body jerks. Her expression slips into that vulnerable look I love. I fuck her clit with my fingers until her sighs taper off. Then I just lay my hand over her entire pussy area and hold her.

Finally, she can speak. "That was epic."

Her voice is so happy, appreciative, satisfied that I admit my manhood takes another good hard solid stroking. It's not about me, but I benefit. Nothing like getting a woman off to the point where she can't speak for a bit.

"I can't get enough of you," I whisper in a lusty, hoarse voice.

"I don't ever want to get enough of you."

That sentence fills me up with hope as I hold her in the afterglow. The sun is beating down on our sweaty bodies, the sea re-announcing itself to us with each crash on the shore. If this isn't bliss, I don't know what is.

"I could fall asleep," she whispers. "That made me really sleepy."

"Could you fall asleep in my arms? Will you?"

"Mmmm," she slurs. "How are you so amazing for someone so young?"

"Please," I ask again.

"I'll try. I'm pretty close with ..." her voice trails off and I hold her snugly.

#

An hour and a half later, she stirs against me and we both wake. I hadn't thought I'd be able to fall asleep with that raging boner, but after like maybe fifteen minutes of listening to her breathe, hearing the waves, and the wind, I apparently conked out too. My eyelids had fluttered closed just as easily as hers.

She stretches and releases a delicious little sexy groan. "Mmmm. Damn. Post orgasm power naps are the best." Her wiggle wakes my lust up like a bear.

I'm grateful she doesn't sit up yet. My cock starts to fill again.

"Well, you are awake, and need to get yours now." She strokes my forearm lightly.

"Ruan, I want you to edge me. I don't want to come until we are on the beach tonight. Deal?"

She pouts. "What? Why? I wanted to get your cum."

"Oh, you will. I just really want it to be built up for tonight. It's been a fantasy of mine to fuck you on the beach ever since we talked about it at the cabin. I want it to be maxed out."

"Okay, I guess I understand." Her lower lip plumps.

Dang. Why is her pouting so damn sexy?

She sits up and I immediately miss her body weight on my cock.

She runs a hand through her lush curls. "Maybe we should shower before dinner. My hair is all knotted up from the beach wind."

"Yes. You go first." I stroke her hair and she sighs sweetly. "But I love your beach hair."

Her jaw drops. "You aren't coming in with me?"

"No. I will come if I step into a shower with you," I laugh out loud. I want to savor this beach fuck fantasy for as long as I can. You shower. I'll shower. Separately. Then we eat, drink, and be merry. And then we fuck each other silly and rotten under the stars."

"Alright, Mr. Romantic," she says with teasing sarcasm and a finger jab between my pecs. "I'll buy into your fantasy, but only because it's yours, and not because I don't want to doggy-back fuck you to explosion in the shower."

I chuckle. "Doggy-back?"

"Yeah, you know, when the woman rides the cock backward during doggy."

"You made that phrase up."

"Yeah, so?" She laughs. "It's accurate, right?"

"Yes. It is. I must say I like it."

The hot shower is luxurious, though painfully lonely knowing she's just in the other room. The water beating my skin is of good force and heat, one of those expensive big, sunflower-like shower heads. Images of Ruan 'doggy-back' fucking me flood my brain and fill my cock full with blood.

"Damn," I mutter. "Edging hurts." I chuckle as I take a few strokes across my hard cock.

Ruan comes in and glances my way. "Damn! Look at you! Waste of good cock. Just saying." She shakes her head, flashes me her naked body before closing her robe and tying it.

"Oh, damn. You trying to get my cock to strangle me to blue balls?"

"Honey, that's your doing. I was ready to fuck you to spill in the shower, remember? It was your idea to wait."

My turn to pout. "Don't make me chase you down and tackle fuck you, cause the way you're going, I'm about to abandon my edging plan and take you all over this cabin like the whore you are."

"Oh, please do! I want that, goofball." She flashes me her bare ass. "Come get me."

I sigh. "Well, that ain't helping." My cock is raging and with Ruan's pussy mere feet from me, bare beneath her robe, and wet as fuck no doubt, my resolve is melting. An odd sense of relief floods me as she leaves.

I finish rinsing, then dash from the bathroom, still dripping wet, and dry off alone in the bedroom. I can't look at her anymore or I'll surely bend her over the bathroom counter and take her to ten orgasms. I dress quickly in dress shorts and a dark green and pink flowered button-up Hawaiian shirt.

She grins at me as she exits the bathroom, drops her robe to the floor, and swings her ass my way. She sashays her hips as she walks and hums. "Tempted?"

"Fuck!" I run from the room, her laughter following me.

A few minutes later, she appears on the deck in a flesh-colored dress with spaghetti straps and a hem that barely covers her ass. Her nipples are hard and protruding out of the fabric, proving she's braless. The dress hugs her curves so well that, from a distance, I'm betting she likely looks naked.

I release a slow whistle. "Damn, babe. You look utterly gorgeous in that dress." I pull her to me as she beams a smile up at my face. I slip my hand down the svelte curve of her hip. "No bra. And no panties."

"Nope. None."

"Shit. This is going to be a very tough meal, knowing you are naked underneath." I press my hard cock to her body. "You are fucking killing me here."

She bites her lip and takes a step back. She grabs my hand and pulls me back into the beach house. "Let's go. Our reservation is getting close."

"And I love the bright red heels, by the way."

"Thank you," she says sweetly. "I thought you'd like them."

She knows my fetish for heels well. They are the last thing I see before I cover my eyes with my free hand. I let her guide me through the beach house. "Take me. If I look at you inside this beach house, I will cave and fuck you. Get me out of here quick," I plead.

#

"Dinner was delicious," I say as I swing her hand, the ocean breeze licking our skin, whipping her blond spiral curls all about like flames of fire. The pier is moderately filled with walkers. We reach the end of it and lean on the rail. "I'm having so much fun with you, Ruan." I hesitate to say more as I examine her eyes first.

"You picked a good restaurant. Thanks again for taking the time to research the area. I had meant to, but I got so bogged down with work that it slipped my to-do list."

She looks relaxed. Happy. I don't want to ruin that.

I clasp my hands together and bounce them up and down.

"You nervous?" She snakes an arm through mine, her hand joins my folded ones. She reaches with her other hand to give my conjoined hands a squeeze.

I take a deep breath and accept my regret before it's out there. "You know I adore being with you, right?"

"Yes, Sebastian. And I adore being with you." Her eyes twinkle in the sinking sunlight.

"And we have fun together, right?"

"Yes, my sweet, sexy man, we do."

She presses her nearest bare breast to my skin and I lose my train of thought.

"Um." I clear my throat, swallow and continue on with my point. "And we are clearly sexually attracted to each other, and compatible."

"Yes again, my hunk of hunk of a man." She squints her eyes at me. "Where is this going, if I dare ask?"

I'm silent for too long. "What if we made us more ... solid?"

"Oh, we are definitely solid." She giggles and checks my crotch with her other hand. She nods. "Yep! Solid. Let's go fuck."

She spins and starts off down the pier, with me in tow, as if she has a rope on me.

"It will be dark in no time. We should go get a little more drunk before our beach fuck."

"Ruan?"

"Yes, my dear?" She stops and looks me in the eye, all expectant and exuberant.

After thirty seconds of silence, I chicken out. I suppress a sigh. I can't age myself any more than I can make her feel I'm worthy of her, which really, I'm not. I'm the lucky one to be with her. Besides, I can't dash that glow in her eyes. I bite back all my feelings even though I know they will fester. I gather all my strength to give her a sexy smile. "I can't wait to fuck you into oblivion on the beach. I've got a plan that will pleasure you into so many orgasms you will be both drunk on sex hormones and shrieks of pleasure." I sigh, disappointed with myself.

"You say the best things, Sebastian."

I can't stay solemn, though, with how alive and vibrant she is now. I can sink into this moment and savor her.

We walk to the car, both smiling, touching, and giving each other charged up fuck-me eyes.

The ride home consists of me riding my hand up her thigh to her pussy to work her clit. She pulls her dress down to expose her breasts and I find it a struggle to keep my eyes on the road.

"I wanna edge you, baby," she utters as she undoes her seatbelt and crawls over my lap. "Can I suck it? I want to give you road head."

"Oh, well fuck, Ruan baby, I'd love it. I'm glad there aren't too many cars on the road."

She undoes my button and unzips my pants. She pulls my cock out with super speed.

"Mmmm. This looks like the best dessert a girl could ask for."

"Now, Ru, don't go crazy and wreck our plan here." My nerves are bunching up something fierce.

"You are my captive now, mister." Her eyes are determined and wanton.

Who could say no to that!

She takes my firm cockhead in her mouth, and I throw my head back to the headrest with a groan.

"Oh, fuck me!" I focus my eyes on the road as I squirm and writhe beneath her.

Her head taps the steering wheel, so I reach down and scoot my seat back a little bit to give her more room.

"That better, babe?"

"Mmm-hmmm," she says with her mouth full of me.

Her humming vibrations send shockwaves through my cock that almost push me over the edge. I'm so jacked I'm getting ready to burst.

"Okay. Okay. Whew! Slow down there, hoover."

She chuckles with me in her mouth and the vibrations again push me even closer to the edge of my climax.

"This is dangerous edging here," I manage to say, though with great effort. Her mouth sounds alone as she sucks me drive me to the edge.

She pops off my cock with a loud smack. "Salty."

I try to regain control of my breathing. "Whew! I thought I was going to lose it there."

She screws her face into a silly expression. "That's the point, Romeo."

"Well, usually I agree." My cock throbs as it dries in the air. "I love smelling like your saliva and my cum, but I really am sticking to my plan of extreme beach fucking here."

"Such a planner this time. I'm used to you just ravaging me room to room non-stop like the stallion you are, not this edging business," she says in a teasing voice.

"Oh, after tonight, watch out. I'm going to be relentless."

"You are being more grown-up about this than me!"

The rest of the way home we cool the sex stuff. We chat about doing a bit of sightseeing, checking out the aquarium, and even an amusement park, so we aren't just all about sex. There's proof. I think it's extra important we do these things. It will show her I'm not just a sex fling.

Chapter Five
Ruan

I walk carefully across the carpet carrying two excessively full glasses of wine, super grateful to have the heels off. They are sexy to wear but hurt like a motherfucker in a hot minute. The carpet feels plush beneath my toes. I slow for a moment to tangle my painted piggies in it while I gaze upon Sebastian sitting on the deck in the lounge chair, his back to me, his lush dark hair flapping in the wind, his strong muscular arm hanging off the armrest. He's just luscious. A gift.

I smile as I shove the pesky twang of guilt to the bottom of my brain, to stew in the other discarded dark thoughts I relegate to down there. Drown and get punished there, why don't you, bad thoughts. Sebastian and I can enjoy each other if we want to, and I'm so thankful we do. For the moment, at least, age doesn't matter. I sniff the rich, heady aroma of the red wine and sigh.

The sky is darkening, but the streams of brilliant pink sunset are shedding their magical hues across the sky, coloring the ocean in its imprint like a fuzzy mirror reflecting an abstract painting. I fear our relationship is deepening, but can my psyche handle that?

"Need help?" he calls over his left shoulder with a glance. His profile is Romanesque with that nose and chin line.

I shake those bad thoughts further away and grin. He will most surely help me feel on the inside what I'm grinning about on the outside. It's better if the two match, so I'm not faking anything with him. That's not fair to him, or me.

"I'm good. I'm coming." I gingerly pad along the carpet so as not to spill red wine on the light beige carpeting.

"Not yet you aren't," he says with a hefty chuckle.

"Oh, I knew that joke was coming." His usual cheesy sex line.

"And again, not yet." He grins as he takes the wine glass from me. "This is a gorgeous sunset. I think I could live here."

"Same." I take a sip of wine, savor it for a moment, then swallow before I sit in the lounge chair next to him. "It's breathtaking."

"Maybe we need a night of sunset fucking too."

I scoff. "True. We've got six more nights after this one, so I'm sure that's something we can add to the list." I trace the tattoo on his bicep with my forefinger, and he smiles at me.

"I'm so happy I found someone to work for me Thursday and Friday. I'd have had to call in sick if I hadn't, I couldn't stand not being here with you when you are here in Florida."

"Me too. I would have been so sad. Well, I would have gotten some work done, but I'd rather spend the whole week fucking you. I get enough work done the rest of the year."

"Yeah," he says in a slow, savoring slur. "Plus, I can show you around a bit and play tourist. I don't do it enough on my own, but showing you my state will be great fun."

I run my fingers down his forearm and tangle my hand in his. He smiles even deeper at me.

"I'm gonna fuck you so hard soon." He points down to the sand. "Right down there in the sand. I'm gonna be ramming your pussy from behind like a mad man."

He says it with such conviction and desire that a surge of lust jolts right through me.

I gasp, then shudder as I recall our intense sexual encounters in the past. He's not wrong in his promises and I love it. Need it.

He chuckles. "Oh, damn, that struck a chord."

I release a pent-up sigh. "Oh boy, did it ever," I whisper as I gaze into his horny charged eyes.

"I've got a plan. I'm going to make you come in front of all the ocean to see. Multiple times. I'm thinking like twenty to thirty times."

His dirty talk always inflames my passion. This is something that has grown over all our interactions over the past year, mostly online, but for the one special time where we got to fuck in person. For a relationship that started online, our intimacy has grown by leaps and bounds. It has grown ever since that Colorado cabin weekend, where our epic fucking was born. Recalling the depth of sexual bliss we took from each other's bodies makes me catch my breath as I swim in the look of burning lust, and more, something I can't quite name, in his gaze. I give it back to him with my eyes and he scoops my head to his for a kiss before laying his lips solidly on mine. Our French kiss deepens as the erogenous zones of my lust rage.

The drone of the ocean waves, the rich wine, his dirty words, and our exquisite kissing are the perfect combo aphrodisiac to a night of fucking, one I don't think either of us will ever forget.

I moan into his mouth as he rides his tongue along mine. Our tongues caress, we suck and fondle for several minutes.

He pulls back. "Whew! As if I wasn't horny as fuck before!"

I take another draw from my wine, wanting to keep this heady swirling going in me. Mix in some orgasms and I'll be flying amongst the stars. I take another big sip, almost a dang gulp, as I maintain eye contact with him.

"Yeah. I'm raging too."

We kiss again, taste the wine off each other's tongues. The wind whips us, and my hair thrashes his head and shoulders in tune with its undulating forces.

He takes my wine glass from me and places it next to his on the end table beside him. He took the liberty of rearranging the deck furniture while I was getting the wine so that our lounge chairs are now touching.

I writhe against his gropes as his hands roam my body from my breasts, down my sides, to my hips and ass cheeks. I can't get enough of touching his shoulders, his pecks, and his tight flat stomach. He's delicious for my fingers. I play around near the waist of his shorts and poke my fingers inside. He grins at me.

"You tease," he mutters.

"Promises, promises. Promises that deliver." I pucker my lips and kiss the air towards him.

"You're mine this round," he says with absolute conviction. "Going to have you my way, and hard. You ready for that?"

"Oh, fuck yes, I am. I've been fantasizing about it for months, ever since Colorado."

"Same. Now." He reaches under his lounge chair and pulls out the spreader. He waves it in the air, the ankle and wrist straps flap slightly. "Ready for this wand to do some magic on your body?"

My heart flutters and my gut lurches. I'm terrified and electrified at once. I nod as my heart pounds. This will be a new experience for me to be somewhat immobile while being fucked. I've literally never gone here with any other lover ever. But it makes sense to do it with Sebastian. Number one, he bought it to bring here to use with me, so I don't want to disappoint, and number two, we've always experimented with each other, so this just fits us. But damn, my nerves are on edge and with how much wine I've drunk, I didn't expect this wobbling of emotions being on the cusp of using it.

"I'm suddenly very thankful I stretch and do yoga."

His stare into my eyes is poignant and aggressive. "Going to bend you over, hold you up by your hips, and fuck your wet, hungry, wanton pussy until you scream into the ocean waves."

I sigh as my heartbeat pounds, even in my toes. "Let's do it." I chug the rest of my wine and stand up. "The anticipation is killing me."

"Sit," he commands. "I'm in control." He clears his throat. "Might be caveman of me, but I'm carrying you down to our fuck spot. And make no mistake, I've already scoped out the perfect spot."

"Wow, you know how to make a woman feel wanted." I giggle and let my head fall to the side. I raise an eyebrow. "Okay. If you want to carry me, I'm all good with that. To be honest, I kinda like you going all caveman like this. Turns me the fuck on." A girl likes to feel taken, claimed, so desired that aggressiveness spews out of her man with great passion and conviction. Sexual confidence is so sexy as fuck. That's why erotica sells. We all want to feel that, even if we only get it through characters. I have a strong feeling this upcoming sexual encounter will be going in my next novel.

My heart continues to flutter as I obey and settle back on the lounge chair as he prepares himself to pick me up. The act seems a bit silly since I was just standing but being scooped up by your lover to go fuck, there's some romantic magic in that act.

He lays the spreader bar across my torso. "Your duty is to carry your restraint." His gaze is so direct, so commanding, my clit responds with a solid twitch.

I hug the bar to my body as he sneaks his arms under my knees and my upper back. He lifts me easily and I release a squeal.

"Oh my!" I say as he spins me quickly to face the deck stairs.

I had snagged the gorgeous beach house with a week rental when the couple who owns it had it reduced in price. I got such a deal, and the actual property has not disappointed at all from the pictures online. For some reason, this particular week was not getting booked, so they had decided to reduce the price for a few weeks to see if they could drum up a booking. Bam, it was right when I had started seriously looking. It had been just after coming home from Colorado, where Sebastian and I had hit it off so well. If I'm being honest, I didn't think we'd click that well in person, but we meshed even better than I had dreamt we would. He totally changed my mind about an age gap fling, and he's continuing to do that.

He holds my eye contact as he carries me across the deck. The waves continue to crash and call out to us to come down and give them a good fuck show.

He gingerly carries me down the stairs, sort of in slow motion. The heat of his taut body melds with mine as I snuggle into him.

"Be a good brute and fuck the shit out of me, will ya?" I mutter into his skin before I suckle his shoulder.

"Oh, I intend to, Ruan." He turns his head and makes an ape-like call out into the darkness, probably a bit too loudly. "I'm going to fuck you better than your male characters fuck their partners in your erotica. I intend to inspire lots of stories in you this week."

"Oh, please do, the thoughts are making my pussy lips slick."

"I love your pussy lips slick." He licks his lips.

He juggles me across the sand with a bit more effort. He grunts for added brute effect.

I giggle. "You can grab me by the hair, just don't pull me through the sand."

He chuckles with a fiery gleam in his eyes. "Don't tempt me, woman." He huffs out another few grunts while swaying me as he walks.

I shriek out as he thrashes my body to and fro.

He pretends to drop me, and I scream out.

"Oh, my gawd," I exclaim with glee, and he snuggles me close to his body.

He grunts exaggeratedly and I can't stop laughing.

He sets me down in the sand and rips my dress off over my head in one fell swoop. It gets hung up on the hand I'm holding the spreader bar with and seductively hangs there. Being bared naked in a semi-public place like this beach thrills me, and the dramatic way he did it only enflames my lust for him further. He rashly tugs my body into position. He grabs for the spreader bar, taking a swing to graze my right nipple in the process. My dress falls to the sand like a long unwanted piece of dried grass, and just as useless.

The waves undulate against the sand, the water penetrating the sand with each stroke, the ocean roar like a moan.

"It's like the ocean is making love to the sand," I whisper.

He presses his body to my backside, his cock a solid, thick rod, his breath bathing my shoulder before he plants a kiss. He pushes my hair out of the way and kisses the back of my neck and continues open-mouth kissing his way down to my middle back. He reaches around to fondle my breasts as he hard presses his manhood against me again. He sways us to the beat of the sea crashing as his hands grope me from behind. I reach back to grasp him before I lose the ability to touch him. I barely get a grope in before he places his palm between my shoulder blades and presses me forward, hard.

I gasp. My hands hit sand.

He roughly grabs my hips and grinds his hard cock against my ass cheeks.

"Oh, fuck," I say with a moan.

He lowers himself behind me and straps my ankles into the restraints on the spreader bar. The act of him securing me is much more erotic than I expected. He reaches between my legs and pulls my right arm between my legs. He tightens the straps around my wrist. As he grabs for my other hand, he brushes his tongue along my inner thigh.

"I can smell your yummy pussy."

He kisses my other hand before he secures it in the wrist restraint too. With all my limbs secured together like I'm a version of hog-tied, my body sways slightly. He steadies my hips with his strong hands.

The vulnerability of my body being open to him is more intoxicating than I had fantasized it would be. My pussy is positively swimming in wetness.

There's a long pause before I watch his shorts and underwear fall to the sand, followed by his shirt. He lines up his bare feet near mine and I relish his stance behind me. His aura of power to dominate me is so sensually erotic, it's dream-like.

I draw in a deep breath and slowly release it as he rides his cock against the crack in my ass cheeks. His cock is hard, packed solid as he rides my skin, lubed by his precum, no doubt.

"Fuck, this is erotic," I mutter as I watch my hair tickle the sand.

He pauses his grinding his skin on mine to grope my ass, hips, and the front of my thighs. "Yes, babe. It is."

With his pelvis firmly pressed to my behind, he reaches one hand around and plays his fingers along my vaginal slit, swiping my juices all along my vulva lips.

"Fuck, babe, you are crazy wet!"

"Mmmm, I know, right? You've got me in a sexed-up frenzy," I murmur dreamily. "I need that cock in me soon or I'll die from want."

He scoffs. "Well, you won't have to wait long, babe."

He presses his fingers into my pussy and I moan out. My eyes close and open as he rolls me into a hotter state by pressing and rubbing my clit.

"Oh, fuck, I want you, Sebastian. Please," I plead as I open my eyes. Down along the beach a ways, I see a couple walking away from us through the strands of my hair flapping in the wind. The thought that they potentially just walked past us and watched us set up like this sends a wave of passion through me, which floods every cell of my being with sexual savoring. I silently urge them to return and just watch Sebastian fuck me into oblivion.

My panting is already out of control as I gasp. As he pumps his fingers into me, the abnormally loud sloshing sounds of them riding my wet hole ring in my ears. I smile. My ears aren't usually so close to my pussy. So, this is what he hears when he's finger fucking me with his head between my thighs.

"Mmmm, fuck fuck fuck," I whisper.

The ocean breeze adds to the eroticism as my body sensations roll along, easily sliding over the hills of our foreplay. A good beach fuck should be sensual, and this is off the charts euphoric, and I haven't even come yet.

He blasts my clit with spanks and moans and sighs fly out of my open mouth. He militantly fucks my womanhood with his fingers, asserting his dominance over owning me. It wets me as my groans grow wild and beastly.

In a gruff voice, he asserts, "I'm gonna fuck you now until you scream into the sand, Ruan. Get ready because I'm not holding back."

I struggle to breathe as I nod, but I'm sure he didn't even notice the movement of my head because he's already pressing the head of his cock into me.

His first thrust is gutsy, bold, and vigorous, so I am assured he's not kidding about his intent to rage fuck me. I'm certain I couldn't even speak if I wanted to.

He bumps my ass with his lower abdomen on repeat as he pounds into me roughly. He smacks my buttocks three times hard with his open hand while still pounding me.

I gasp as he sends my ass cheeks bouncing with each slam into me, my boobs flap wildly back and forth as he all-out obliterates my pussy with unapologetic mad fucking. He spanks me a few more times with a manly grunt and I melt further into getting lost in my climbing pleasure.

I moan and whimper as hunger erupts in me like panic, my ability to keep my sounds inside proving to be impossible. "Oh, my gawd, oh, my gawd, oh fuck ..." I barely get it out before I scream.

Our amorousness matches as we both let our sounds of fervor rip into the night.

He doesn't slow his slamming into me as I burst over the edge of my climax and plunge into it so hard, harder than I ever thought I could. The bar prevents my usual body curl from happening, but the force of the orgasm is still trying to move my body so the whole feeling of the orgasm is intensified.

"Fuck," I scream out before I fall fully silent. I can't breathe as my vaginal muscles contract so forcefully on his cock that it almost hurts. Squeeze after squeeze, I lose count after nine contractions. Finally, the high subsides a bit so I can release the moan that was stuck in me when my breath wouldn't flow out.

"Oh, gawd, oh gawd, oh my gawd," I utter as he still wallops himself against my ass cheeks, plunging his erection deep into me. My climax rolls instead of plummets and his fucking of me sends me rising again. My climax unlatches and I am thrown into a second orgasm, an impossibly even more intense one. I screech, moan, and gutturally groan my way quickly to the top of it and my body is flung into another strong orgasmic thrashing. My clit might command me, but he rules my clit.

He continues to bludgeon my body with his until I've reached somewhere near fifteen orgasms, but I've lost count. I am beyond the flaccidity of a rag doll when he slows his pumping into me and reaches down to release my wrists from the bondage. The relief is real but so is the eroticism, and I can't get enough of him guiding me through this fuck session.

He gives a simple push to my hip. I fall forward towards the sand. His bold shove crumples me and I land face down in the sand, my knees hit the ground, keeping my ass up. I yearn to lie flat, my thighs already held open for him to barrage me further, but he steadies me into the position of a kneeling doggy fuck before I can even shift. I'm weak and want to lay down, but I lift my face out of the sand, brush the grains off my sweaty skin as best as I can, prepare myself for what deliciousness is yet to come. As I prop myself up on my elbows, he roughly enters my pussy.

His deep gruff groan as he penetrates me fills the deep desire in me to sexually fulfill him.

The next orgasm I have is weaker, but still yummy in its own right. He speeds up his fucking of me, his aggressive thwacks telling me he's close to coming. His guttural sounds are so loud, I imagine his face is pointed toward the moon as if he were a wolf howling at it, and just as aggressive and wild as one.

Deep satisfaction fills me as I savor the blast of his cum inside me, and the immediate birth to the slosh of our sex fluids mixing inside me. He stirs up our cum together as he slowly rides his waning cock in and out of me.

"Oh. Dear. Gawd." The influx of sex hormones has me drunker than I am. All I want to do is crash into the still-warm sand, hold my body to his under the inky fusion of the sky with the bright brilliant rims of each star blazing down on us.

I fall because I'm too spent to stay up anymore. He crashes into the sand next to me, landing with a thud. We snuggle into each other, slightly writhing until we get to the most comfortable union of our bodies, not a care for the fact that we are both naked and our skin is getting covered in a coating of sand.

Our bodies are so tightly packed together it's like we are woven together. Or perhaps, that's just our sexual energies blended to perfection.

Chapter Six
Sebastian

I don't think I've ever fucked anyone that hard in my entire life. My breath has still not returned to normal. It wasn't just like we just had sex on the beach, it was like we had a lifetime of epic sex on the beach. Like it's something never to be topped. My beast mode came out like a monster-beast from the fiery lust pits of hell itself. Part of me is terrified that I scared her, the other part is thrilled how many times it seems she came. Neither of us has spoken since we broke the union of our fuck. We are both simply breathing, mine still more labored cause of free-freak mode happening. I even shocked myself.

I sneak a peek at her face. I don't think she's asleep, but I can't say for sure.

The warm breeze off the sea is still warm, so neither of us are shivering. The temptation to sleep like this is irresistible. I don't plan on moving until she does.

"Sebastian?" she asks in a sweet voice.

"Yes, babe?" I can't help it, my heart races.

"That was the most amazing sex I've ever had in my life. You demolished me. I think I came twenty-one times, but, honestly, it was really hard to count. I was kind of out of it for part of it."

I laugh, which sounds more like a sigh, because that's what it really is. "No shit? Wow! That's epic! That excites me, Ruan." Relief floods me.

She snuggles back in against me and again, I don't want to move a muscle. I want to live the rest of my life just like this, here, holding her sexually satisfied body to mine, eating up the calming crashing of the waves, the light hum of a gentle breeze. Surely this is sexual bliss, on top of regular bliss. As near as possible to what living in constant euphoria must feel like.

"I went a little bit over the top caveman, didn't I? I feel like I should beat my chest or something." I give a curt, nervous laugh.

"Oh, fuck no. You raged me so hard I came so hard and so often. It was beyond cloud nine status. Easily the best sexual experience of my entire life."

I didn't think more relief was possible, but it fills every sweaty crack inside and outside of my body. I sigh deeply, then a wild laugh spurts out. "Careful, I don't need bigger a head than I already have."

She reaches over and squeezes my cock head, which is still throbbing a bit, so I squirm and yell out.

She giggles and drops my cock. "Such a nice big cockhead it is too."

It lands as a semi against my belly, having started to thicken when she had touched it.

"I've been getting aftershocks. It's like my whole body is sighing. I'm tingling like I've been riding an old shaky tractor for hours."

"Yeah, that means great out-of-the-world sex, babe."

"No shit. I can't wait to write this scene out for a book."

"Oh yeah? I'm really happy to hear that. I love the idea of being your sexual writing muse."

"You definitely are and have been already."

"I know, right? I have loved seeing bits and pieces of us in your last book. That was killer awesome."

"I love to do that. It's like … our sex … is immortalized."

"Yeah, wow. I never thought of it that way. But you are so right."

"I'd love to get this spreader off, though, so I can move my legs freely." She sits up but I beat her to removing the ankle restraints.

"Going to need to rinse this thing off." I lay the bar diagonally along my lower torso and groin. "We got it excessively coated with sand. As has my ass crack."

"I think we've gotten everything coated with sand. And yeah, so much for not getting sand in the ass crack. I think I'm in the same boat as you since I laid down." She laughs heartily, and it warms my heart.

I join in her laughter before I say, "Yeah, I can feel the little grains creeping into my ass as we speak."

"No, that's the sand beetles."

I squawk and sit up. "What? Serious?"

She's cracking up so hard it warms my heart. Finally, after her hysteria calms, she says, "We will need a shower before bed. Gotta get the ass cracks clean, so we don't spill sand in the bed. I hate that."

"I'll gladly wash your ass crack," I chime in.

"Oh, I just bet you would," she says haughtily. "Shit, I just can't get over it. That was the most sensually rough fuck of my entire life. You just slayed me."

"It will be memorable for life for me." Oh, well shit. I might as well just ask. "I didn't scare you, did I? Was I too rough?"

"No. Definitely not. A woman loves to be ravished. Well, at least I do, can't say all women, but many do."

"I'm just reeling too. That was so intense. I have to admit, I scared myself a little bit."

"Same. And not sure we can top that ever."

"Oh? Well, I fully accept that challenge to top it, even if I have to spend my whole life trying, it will happen."

Her silence that follows seems a bit ominous, but I shove those feelings aside, I'm not letting anything ruin this moment with her. I have her in my arms, our bodies are spent from pleasuring each other to the max, and my plan has succeeded in making reality even better than the fantasy. That's no small thing.

"I believe we will sleep damn well tonight. What an epic first day we've had."

"Yeah, I kind of feel like we've already had like four days together. Not complaining at all." I squeeze her despite my fears that the week will be over before we know it.

"No doubt." She sighs. "The moon and the stars are so bright and beautiful."

"Just like you."

She scoffs. "I love it when you get sappy romantic." She traces my sand-covered chest and right nipple, the coarse grains off her fingers mildly biting into my skin. "That was some daredevil sex. I wonder if anyone saw us. I noticed a couple off in the distance when we first started."

I chuckle devilishly. "Ruan, they walked right past us. They actually nodded and smiled at me. I had half a mind at the time to invite them to stay and watch."

Her hand flies to cover her mouth. "Oh! Are you serious? Oh, my gawd!"

"Yep. That would have heightened it for me even further had they watched. Maybe they would have fucked right alongside us. Could you imagine?"

"Oh, damn, that's hot as fuck. Okay, that's going in the story when I write it." She slaps my chest with her hand. "Damn good idea!"

"I should have done it." I sigh through my smile. "They were an older couple, but clearly very sexually open."

"I bet the neighbors saw. That's hot too."

"I know. I had that thought as well. At one point, the house over on the right had their outside light on, then it went off. I bet they saw something of us."

"I love that. It makes the memory of it even more delicious."

"I'd love to sleep out here, but we might get cold at some point. And honestly, I'm hungry as a horse after fucking you like that. Should we head in?"

"Yep, I could use a snack too."

We peel ourselves out of the sand and each brush off as much as we can.

"The sweat makes it stick like glue." She whacks at her hips.

"Mmm, I wouldn't mind doing that to you. Bend over." I chuckle with my spanking hand at the ready.

She just laughs and keeps brushing the sand off her creamy skin.

"I think I might have left a handprint, I smacked you so hard one of those spanks." I try to get a glimpse of her ass and she rotates so I get a full view.

"See one?" she asks jovially. "If not, you might need to try again another day."

"Oh, I'm up for that challenge."

We both laugh as we trudge through the sand to the deck stairs.

Once inside, the bright light shows how beautiful her eyes are after being fully fucked into satisfaction. They dance with flirtatious delight as she pulls me along to the shower. She's so fucking hot, my cock fills as she tugs me across the living room.

"Oh, damn. Look at that thing. You haven't had enough yet. Well, I'm up for a shower quickie if you are."

I hadn't expected this with how much we've played today, but who's going to not use a boner when they are with the woman they are in love with? Certainly not me. I need to get my fill to last until our next getaway. I stop cold. Did I just really think that? Oh, fuck. I need a change of subject to think about, quick.

"Hey, where will we go next? I like to have something to look forward to." I panic, thinking she can read the love in my eyes.

She smiles sheepishly at me as she turns on the shower. "Well, I was thinking it might be fun to go somewhere up north or to Canada this summer. Like on a lake. Do you think we can get more time off to come? I'll buy your plane ticket if you can't swing it. I know it's kind of soon." She snakes her hands around me. "Do you fish?"

I smile, deeply pleased that she's obviously thought about this already. "If we plan it, I will make it happen for sure. And, yes, I fish."

We step into the shower. The blast of the hot water makes us both sigh.

"This feels amazing. Now bend over, I'm going to wash your ass crack."

"Hey, I thought I was washing your ass crack."

"Let's take turns," I insist. "You first."

"Well, if you go first washing me, I don't think we will get to washing yours before we are fucking again."

I grin. "And your point is?"

I rub the soapy washcloth all over her generous breasts, spending extra time washing her nipples. "Gritty sand is my excuse." She rubs her soapy hands all over my arms and biceps, traveling her hands along my chest and stomach, and briefly visiting my cock for a few strokes as a smile lives on her face.

"We might get sore with all this sex."

"Never a better reason to get sore than too much sex!"

The water beats on my back as I spin her to face away from me. I run my soapy fingers along her ass crack. I return my attention to her front as I run the washcloth over her tummy and generously lather up her pussy, much to her delight. She moans and lays against me as I rub the wet cloth over her clit nub.

"Mmmm, how am I getting so aroused again?"

"You aren't alone. I'm getting hot too." I press my full erection to her back and glide it along her wet skin.

Next. I soap up her hair. "I want to bathe you sometime. Ever been bathed by a lover?"

She shakes her head as I massage the shampoo into her hair. I place her right under the water stream and help press the suds out of her strands of hair with my hands. As I apply the conditioner, she moans out her pleasure.

"I love your hands in my hair. It feels so good."

"I love your hair. Your curls are beautiful."

Her hair clings to her supple skin in thick wet sections. I spin her to face the side of the shower stall, so the water hits her side. I soap up my hand and rub the soap bubbles into her ass crack again, making sure to lightly caress over the pucker of her anus, and to spread the soap along her perineum, then up over to wash her slit again.

She laughs. "My pussy is pretty clean now." She says, "Mmm, as is my ass."

I chuckle too. "Oh, it's never too clean."

I run soap down my body and legs before I do the same to her.

"Ready for a quick fuck?" I ask hopefully.

She obliges with a nod and an enthusiastic exclamation, "Yes!"

I bend her slightly over and she grips the shower wall with both palms spread wide open. I press into her and ride her as the water streams across our bodies, our moans bouncing off the walls. She plays with her clit as I pound her mercilessly from behind again. After she comes, I let mine blow free inside her vagina. A quick fuck after an epic fuck is no less delicious.

We dry off with smiles plastered across our faces.

"This should be illegal. This is way too much fun," I say as I slip into my sleep boxers. I slide a t-shirt over my head. I watch her dress in a red silky nightie, which hugs her curves so well I'm getting aroused again. "Geez, I'm a fucking sex-crazed man, you look so sexy in that."

She grabs my hand. "We need food and water. Then sleep."

After a snack of cheese, crackers, summer sausage, and grapes, we settle into bed and the realization that I've never been happier in my life lets me drift sweetly and swiftly into dreamland, dreaming about tomorrow with Ruan.

#

The morning sun paints the inside of the bedroom in strong rays that lay across her blond hair in new ways as I watch her sleep. How she can look even more beautiful each day to me is beyond a mystery. My morning wood is waiting for her, but I think I'll wake her with oral instead. She's due an orgasm or fifteen from being eaten out. We have plans to visit the aquarium today, get lunch, and then go on a catamaran for the afternoon. A happy hour cruise for adults only, with all the alcoholic beverages we want and appetizers. The day ahead promises to be a dream come true, starting with me waking her by eating her out.

I shift in the bed carefully and slowly, and she doesn't move a muscle. Her eyes are still closed, her breathing still evenly rhythmic.

She stirs slightly as I pull the sheet off her body, perhaps the sudden draft of being without a cover, but luckily, she doesn't fully wake. I'm super thankful she's on her back. I grin devilishly as I gently move her right leg to allow myself to snuggle closer to her pussy. This causes her to shift, but she remains asleep. Perfect! I very carefully lift her nightie up to expose her crotch. I inhale deeply. Oh, how I love the rich, earthy aroma of her bare pussy. I nuzzle my face to part her thighs a little bit further apart. I extend my tongue for the first lick along her closed lips that shield the delicious canyon of her womb beneath. Slipping the tip of my tongue to spread her lips is divine. I press in further and she moans. Her feminine smell blooms as she spreads her thighs apart further to allow me full access to her.

"Mmm, Sebastian?" Her eyes flutter open and I go into her pussy for a full coverage hard suck. "Oh! Omigosh! Oh! Mmmm fuck!" She writhes against my head as I suck her loose flesh. Her hands fly to tangle into my hair. "Holy fuck!" she exclaims. She squirms. The stream of sunlight from the not fully closed blinds lands across her face, highlighting her eyes and making them look cerulean blue. Her plush lips are puckered as her eyes close in accompaniment with a deeply appreciative sounding moan.

I'm not coming off the glans of her clitoris, not breaking that suction until her body coils from orgasming. Her legs move nonstop as I continue to molest her swollen clit head. Come on, baby, let's get you to scream and spill cream for me to lap up. I increase my sucking as her moans grow more insistent, whimpering, frantic. Her body tenses, her legs raise off the bend, her torso curls. I glance up while keeping the suction going and her eyelids flutter as her eyes zone off to the left and upward. Yes! Success!

She finishes her usual pattern of falling silent, then releases a huge gasp, followed by several moans and sighs that taper off. White cream oozes out her lower lips and I quickly swipe my tongue along her flesh to eat it all up. I lick a few more times, pry my tongue inside to scoop out any cum still lingering inside her. I take a swipe up her nub and she startles with a gasp. I drop my mouth on her for a momentary strong suck, then pop off her bean and raise myself up on my elbows.

"Good morning, sunshine. How was that? Starting out with an orgasm while waking up?"

She writhes against me while releasing more sighs and moans. "Wow," she murmurs in a sleepy voice. "That was epic. I thought I was dreaming and then it was real."

If I could package that little satisfied grin of hers, I'd be a millionaire. "You are so fucking sexy, babe. I've dreamt of doing that to you for a long time."

"Oh, it was amazing. I'll have to return the favor sometime."

"Don't hold back. I'm in for that kind of a wake-up call anytime. And every day." I chuckle. "Well, I don't need that every day. Just saying."

"It's on my week's agenda." She stretches and gives a little squeak.

"How do you even make stretching sexy?"

I crawl up to her and pull her on top of me. I tug her head down for a kiss. We give each other a peck.

She flushes. "I need to brush my teeth first."

"Nah. Just kiss me."

She shies away with a curl of her body to the side and slips out of my grasp. "At least a mint?"

"That's all I've got time for. My cock is calling to rock your pussy, so get that mint and let's fuck."

After a scrumptious, intimate, and slow, taking-our-time intercourse fuck, we mosey to the kitchen for a quick breakfast before we need to leave to make our tour on time. She starts up the coffee and I pull out the croissants, cream cheese, strawberries, and pre-cut melon.

"When we go out to eat, I'm buying. You've bought all this food at the house for the week."

"It's okay, Sebastian. I'm not going to bother you for that."

I frown. "I have money, Ruan."

"Oh, I know you do, baby. I just want to treat you."

Part of me loves her for it, but the other part feels shamed. Admonished. "Well, I'm buying lunch for sure."

She pats my hand and smiles. "I got it."

I press my lips together. "I'm no slouch." It's getting hard to not take offense.

"I know you aren't a slouch. You work hard, baby."

It's impossible to not stare at her. The little tight legging-shorts she has on highlight how lusciously round her ass and hips are, it's like the dang garment was made for her body.

Chapter Seven
Ruan

Being in public with Sebastian makes me focus on our age gap, which is not something I am enjoying. I've gotten a few glances I wanted to give the finger to, but most people don't seem to give a shit. I have to wonder if Sebastian notices anything. I mean, I look rather young for my age, but it's obvious Sebastian could be my child, doesn't take much of an age gap for that, really. But the ways he touches me clearly indicate he's not my child. Him calling me 'mommy' while snugging his pelvis up against my ass in the line to get into the dolphin exhibit at the aquarium brought a snarl of disgust from an older woman. I all out had to bite my tongue and turn my head away because I was laughing so hard. Sebastian just grinned and called me, 'mommy' again. The woman swiftly left as Sebastian and I both had cracked up.

"Age prude," I had said as we ushered ourselves into the building.

"Agism is real. Both ways."

Now, sitting at the lunch table, I've all but gotten over it. I had laughed it off, but it also caused a bite. I really only care what I think, and what Sebastian thinks. But I do know I don't want to ruin his life. I refuse to do that. He's way too special to just be a boy toy. He needs a real committed woman. One he can start a family with and be that football dad wearing his son's team jersey on the sidelines and fucking his wife at night while the kids sleep. He needs that normal life. Life with me would not be a normal life. But then, what's normal? There really isn't such a thing as normal. That much I've learned in my lifetime. Mutual consent for everything should be the normal, and that's as far as the label should go. I refuse to wear that judgmental hat.

"I'll bet you the first three orgasms next time we have sex that I know what's going through your mind."

He looks way too serious for my liking, and I have the strong urge to talk about the sharks and tropical fish tanks we just saw to stave off any talking that will come from that mood. I smile before opening my mouth to say something mundane and unimportant about colorful fish, but he beats me to the punch.

"You are thinking about the ugly look that woman gave us earlier."

I press my lips together and blink my eyes before looking directly into his. "Fffftt." No use in denying it. "You got me."

"That's the shit I don't care about, Ruan, babe."

Saved by chance, our waiter appears with our food. "BLT for you, young sir. Caesar salad and minestrone soup for you, miss."

"Thank you. It looks amazing." I beam my sweetest smile at him.

"Great. Thanks."

"I'm starved. You?"

"Yes," he says a bit expectantly.

I feel his gaze focused on me as I avoid his eyes.

"Hey. Let's talk about this. I don't want this between us. Not when we are finally together in person."

"I'm good with it all, Sebastian. Really."

"I'm not okay just dismissing this. Look. I can fuck you six ways from Sunday and paddle your bottom, mommy. I'm not a kid and you know it."

A little smile flickers across my face, like I can't stop it because it owns me. In all honesty, he owns me. "Well, these are things I know."

"Let's get that straight. And I can dom you into an orgasm in no time, so let's keep the agism out of our relationship. Others can take that tone, but we shouldn't. We are both together because we want to be."

I smirk, loving how he's taking charge with vehemence in this conversation. "Well said. Note taken." But, yet, we can't ignore the obvious.

"Good." His grin goes evil. "And I think I want to play out that scenario tonight. I'll hang that swing and get out your paddle. What do you say?"

I turn beet red, which rarely happens. "Well, damn. I get only the naughty role-play option, huh?" I allow my eyes to twinkle with playful lust. "Maybe I didn't bring the paddle."

He raises an eyebrow at me and cocks his head, as if he doesn't believe me for a second. "Damn. My testosterone must be off the charts. It must be from being with you. You make me horny as fuck any and every day, but when we are together, it's like I'm seventeen again."

I shudder as I realize that was only nine years ago for him. "Were you one of those seventeen-year-olds who wanted to fuck your friends' moms?"

"Oh, hell yeah. Weren't we all?" His face glazes over for a second. "Whether a guy talked about it or not, we all did at one point or another. Our brains were hard-wired for constant sexual thoughts."

I laugh. "I get it. I felt that way about a few of my friends' dads at one point." I can't help but wonder if I'm just a fulfillment of that fantasy for him, and nothing more. But regardless, that fits with my mantra, so I shove the worry out of my brain.

He gives me a direct gaze I can't ignore. "We good?"

I nod. "We are good."

"Good. That's what I like to hear."

"We can change at the sailboat place, by the way. They have changing rooms." I dig into my salad with a ferocious stab. "Mm. I'm so hungry."

"Great. Which bikini did you bring?"

"Black."

"Oh, I love the black against your creamy white skin and blond hair. Good choice."

We eat the rest of our lunch chit-chatting about the aquarium and the upcoming sailboat cruise.

#

Sebastian pulls me along the gangplank and onto the boat. The party music is already pumping, and the bartender is already pouring drinks. After lunch, we walked along the beach holding hands, watching the waves, the people swimming, and those sunbathing. It felt so normal, not like two people from different generations; it just felt right. That's a dangerous thought for me to dwell on.

Sebastian's grin is delicious as he pulls me to him once we've boarded. The boat is huge, larger than I had expected for a catamaran. I thought we'd all be standing on top of each other, but it's quite spacious. The sky has cooperated and it's giving us its bright blue sunshine-filled face. Pelicans and seagulls fly about as we wait for the crew to ready for launch.

Sebastian spins me and walks me to the rail. We both look out to the vast sea as he rocks us back and forth as a unit.

"This is a beautiful boat. You are beautiful. We are going to have a blast."

No one has given us a nasty look yet so I'm feeling relaxed. "Yeah. I'm really excited. I've never done anything like this. I bet you have, since you've lived here your whole life."

"Yep, I've done it several times. Which is why I knew I wanted to take you. It's a really good time. I've even been on this exact boat before."

"Really? Oh wow!"

He leans over and plants a kiss on the top of my head, over the part in my hair.

"Yeah. A couple of years ago. You know, all I can think about is ripping this bikini off of you and fucking you into a massive amount of orgasms." He tugs at the hem of my bikini top.

I giggle. "Aw, you say the sweetest things."

A waiter steps near us and says, "Can I get you two a margarita or beer?"

"Yes, I'd love a margarita," I say.

"On the rocks or slushy?" he asks with a sexy grin.

He can't be much off of Sebastian's age and he's sexy as fuck. Being of the sex on the brain nature, my mind goes right to being sandwiched between these two in an epic threesome. I gasp as the full image consumes me.

Something in my expression, or perhaps my eyes, apparently makes him naughty-grin and it's delicious as fuck. Our shared flirt is silent, but solid.

"Slushy please," I reply.

"Original or strawberry?" His smirk deepens, then I watch him make eye contact with Sebastian. Oh, now that's intriguing.

"Original." I return his sexy smirk and let my eyes speak my idea.

"Nice choice, my sexy lady." He turns his gaze to Sebastian. "And you, my lucky man?"

Sebastian chuckles. "Oh, I'm lucky alright. You have no idea."

The waiter laughs. "Oh, I think I might. And, yes, you are a very lucky man indeed." His snicker is unmistakable. He finds us both hot.

Sebastian nods and his motions move my body with his. "Fuck yes, I am. And I'll take what the sexy lady is having as well. Thank you."

"I'll be back in a flash," he says as he blasts us a toothy grin.

I spin to face him, press my breasts against his front. Our skin on skin is heavenly. "Well, that was rather yummy. My mind went naughty, of course."

"A threesome?" he asks with a deep, salacious grin.

"Of course. Would you ever do one?" Oh, he knows me so well.

"Probably. I never have, but I'd be open to it. I'm more into female-female-male myself, but I'd try a threesome, with rules." He shrugs. "I'm not saying I'd not try things, just rather unsure how I'd react."

"Oh, always with rules, definitely." My wheels begin to spin as my lust rages up. "And we never know how we will react until we are in the moment, but, nonetheless, a very interesting idea indeed." My brain launches into a threesome script of the three of us.

The waiter returns with our margaritas and my eyes fall to his crotch, which is pressing out a significant bulge. He catches my glance and nods with a hinting gleam in his eyes.

"Why, thank you, kind sir," I say in a breathy voice while taking the glass from him. Giving him a nickname of power makes my clit twitch. I notice his name tag this time. Juan is giving me the eye strokes along my body big time.

"Thanks, my man," Sebastian says as he takes his plastic cup from the waiter.

"I'm at your service, any time, for any thing this cruise. Don't hesitate to ask." He flashes us that supermodel smile again and walks off.

"You think that was an invite?" I ask excitedly.

"Could be. We'll see how he acts. I'd like to give you that fantasy if you want it." He presses his forehead to mine. "It's a version of mine too, but honestly, I just want to fulfill yours and get you off as hard and as often as possible. I am not into anal, but I'd love to pleasure you up with another man to spoil you as the true sex goddess you are."

"You are perfect bliss, you know that, right?"

He snuggles me close while we both hold our drinks out from our bodies so we can be as close as possible to each other.

When he releases me, we clink our plastic cups together.

"Cheers to more cheers!" I chant.

"Cheers, babe."

We both sip and glance around. Our eyes have been on each other, so we haven't noticed our fellow boat cruisers much yet. There's a big mix of people, some young, some middle-aged, and one gray-haired couple who look like they'd be a blast to hang out with based on their smiles, their laughter, and the way they touch each other in relaxed comfortable, yet intimate ways. A state to aspire to, no doubt.

The drinks flow way too easily and Juan keeps our cups full, actually brimming, with alcohol. Sebastian grabs my hand and we abandon our drinks to dance. Dancing in a bikini is a challenge, but a sexy fun one as my bikini is tending to shift. After twenty minutes of dancing, I'm pretty sure everyone on the boat has at least seen one of my nipples, if not both. Sebastian pretends to faint when I pop a nipple on purpose, and we collapse together laughing.

This time his mouth finds my nipple and it's game on. We kiss, swaying to the music, the alcohol, and warm sun, and bare skin brushes nudging our lust along. Juan is ever the attentive waiter offering us appetizers and more drinks.

I circle my arm around Sebastian's neck and pull his head down so his ear is even with my mouth.

I whisper with my lips brushing his ear, "Let's fuck Juan."

He pulls back and his eyes are surprised and wide, but he's grinning hugely. "Yeah?"

I nod with a devilish grin. "Yeah. Let's do it. We may never get a chance like this again. He's been flirty with us this whole afternoon. And he's been giving me the fuck-me eyes like crazy. I think he'd be on board."

"He's been giving me them too. Ok. I'll consider it. With rules?" He shifts back and forth on his bare feet while looking around the room. "We would have to make sure he's on the same page as us. And I'm not taking dick in any way."

"No one said you had to take it. I'll get it rolling. I'll whisper in his ear." My heart starts to pound. "Make sure he isn't only about dp."

"Right. I know you don't want to do that, so we just need to be clear in our approach. But nothing says we can't both be loving on you."

Even Sebastian looks excited about this prospect. His cock is reacting in his swimsuit. "Okay, if you are in, I say let's do this."

I grab the mound of his cock from outside of his swim trunks and give it a quick squeeze. He's rock hard. I look him in the eyes and bite my lower lip, nod, then spin around so I can locate Juan. People are dancing, gyrating, and standing in line for a pour of alcohol right from a bottle of rum. Everyone appears to be getting smashed. Two women are topless at the front of the boat, waving their bikini tops in the air like lassos. Two more are getting ready to join. Hell, I'd do it if I weren't about to fuck two men. That thought sends shivers of glee throughout my body.

I spot Juan in the back corner of the boat. He's whispering in a woman's ear. The woman is quite sexy, in a bikini with only tiny orange squares that cover her nipples. She's small-breasted, which is why she can get away with wearing that kind of bikini. My melons would shred it. I make a beeline for Juan. When he turns around, I'm right behind him.

"Hi, Juan," I say seductively. "I was wondering if I could tell you a secret."

He grins immediately, and that look of wanton lust fills his eyes.

I do the finger motion to have him bend down. I go up on my tippy toes and ask, "Threesome? Me, you, Sebastian, but no anal for us?"

Juan throws his head back and laughs. It's a belly laugh, but it's so loud on the boat that his laughter is not out of place. In fact, no one even seems to have noticed his explosion.

He nods enthusiastically. "Yes. Yes. Yes. And I will take anal if he so chooses, but I do not need it to enjoy. I mostly want you anyway." He glances over at Sebastian. "Though he is very sexy too, if I'm being honest." He nods towards an area behind a canvas wall. "Meet you back there in a few minutes. I will inform my bartender I will be ... occupied for a bit. He will understand and cover for me." His grin is so sexy I just want to suck it.

I squeal and clap my hands. Dashing for Sebastian, I almost fall as the boat shifts. I grab a chair to steady myself. Or perhaps I'm just drunk as a thirsty skunk.

I make it to Sebastian, my buzz in full effect as I say, "He said yes! And he would be into anal if you want to do it, but he said he doesn't need it."

Sebastian's eyes go blank. "Oh, well shit. I hadn't thought of that."

"Well, you don't have to. But if you've ever wanted to try it, now is your time."

"Fuck. I don't know. Never really desired to do that, but if the guy wants it." He hesitates and his eyes cloud. He shrugs. "What would you think of me if I did try it?"

"Oh, Sebastian, I wouldn't mind at all. Oftentimes I wonder if I'm pan myself. Plus. Dicks can be washed. Or perhaps you should wear a condom. I'll ask him to wear one in me. Wait. Shit. Oh no! We have no condoms! What if he doesn't either?"

"I'd bet good money he has some." Sebastian shrugs. "In any case, I think I need a shot of tequila so I can wake up the testosterone to do this nasty deed." He scoffs. "I really do think I need to be more drunk for this." He shoves both hands in his lush hair. "Can I fuck a man in the ass just because he wants it?"

"It's one fuck, Sebastian. Experimenting doesn't make you that way, you know."

"Oh, I know. I'm not threatened. Just not sure if I could maintain an erection. But then, you will be there, so maybe I could. Aw, fuck. I gotta think about this."

He starts off for the bar in a rush.

"Well, you'd better think quick!" I call after him. "Meet us there!" I realize too late I've yelled this across a group of people. As they glance my way, I just smile and wave. They smile back. We're all drunk here. No one gives a fuck.

I down the rest of my margarita as my pulse races. I tremble as I set down the cup. This will be one of the most epic sexual experiences of my life. My lips slosh together as I walk, my pussy is so extremely aroused and wet. The idea of two cocks and me, two mouths on me, and four hands groping on me is beyond titillating. It's a thing of my fantasies I didn't think I'd ever get to enjoy, and with two younger men. I'm in total fuck-heaven.

As I round the edge of the canvas wall, Juan is naked and stroking his cock pretty hardcore, like it owes him something. His penis is large, swollen, and purplish. And it's beautiful, just like him.

"Wow, holy fuck! You are quite large!" I exclaim.

He chuckles as he releases his cock and it sways.

"That's positively hypnotic!" I can't seem to look away.

"You may touch me," he says in this sexy voice that makes my pussy practically quake.

Sebastian appears before I even move to reach for Juan.

"Um, before we start. Condoms?"

He turns around and bends over, pointing his nice, firm ass my way. He plucks two little squares from the floor, stands up, spins back around, and hands one square to Sebastian. "Sleeve up, my friend, so we can fuck." His grin is positively irresistible. "Waiters with benefits at your service. My ass is yours to enjoy."

Both Sebastian and I crack up. Juan's charm is delectable.

"You've done this before, haven't you, Juan?" I glance at Sebastian, who is also grinning.

"Ah, yes, beautiful lady, I have. People get horny on the boat and I'm open." He tears the condom open with his teeth and pulls out the circular form of the condom. "I get lucky a lot." He raises an eyebrow and gives us a salacious grin. "Let's fuck."

"Allow me?" I ask with raised hands.

"You do me, I'll do him. With your permission, sir?"

Sebastian recoils but then relaxes his shoulders. He shrugs and his expression goes lazy. "When in Rome." He shrugs again and drops his swim trunks. His cock swings out like the beauty it is.

We stand in a triangle, my hands dressing Juan's cock in a condom, Juan's hands unrolling the sheath down Sebastian's erection, and Sebastian's fingers groping my ass, hips, and breasts. Our eyes connect on repeat, the excitement evident in all our gazes. They both close in on me once the cocks are fully in their covers. Their hand motions both become frenzied as they caress and cup my breasts and ass cheeks. They are moving so quickly that I'm overwhelmed already. My breathing speeds up to match theirs. Two cocks pressed to my skin is even more exciting than I had anticipated. My desire is pulled taut, ready to launch, my lust afire.

"Mmm, damn," I moan.

"I'm so juiced for this," Juan mutters as he reaches past me to fondle Sebastian. "Okay with this?"

"Yes," Sebastian says. "I'm doing this for her, but I'm up for anything, except I won't suck your cock and I won't be anally fucked. Otherwise, I'm drunk enough for the rest."

"Excellent," Juan says as he groans. "A sexy woman sandwich with a man like you is my fantasy."

I can tell Sebastian is antsy, fighting his natural tendencies while trying to please me. I'm breathless between them as they voraciously molest my body. The alcohol adds to my exhilarated state and moans spill out of my mouth between ever-increasing panting. I'm so charged up when Sebastian kisses my neck, I flop against him. The air feels electrified as Juan consumes me with a deep French kiss that seems to go on for days. Having a cock pressed to my front and a cock pressed to my back mesmerizes me. I deeply wish I could stay smashed between their hot, writhing bodies. Every touch triggers a roll towards my orgasm peak.

Sebastian works my nipples into stiff nuggets as Juan continues to explore my mouth with his tongue. I follow his lead with my hunger, searching for more of him with my own tongue. Sebastian kisses my neck and shoulders. Two mouths on me make me shudder; it feels so lush and indulgent, hypnotic. My brain explodes with ideas for positions, and I want to do them all.

Juan kisses down my chin, my neck, and on towards my breasts. Sebastian pulls my bikini top off my nipples, exposing them just in time for Juan's mouth to devour my right nipple. He suckles like he means it and I moan, thrash my head against Sebastian's pecks. Juan continually alternates between squeezing my body and groping beyond my body to grab Sebastian. Being literally trapped between two strong men is both mesmerizing and terrifyingly delicious. Their immense masculine strength gets boasted as they, at times, indulge in grabbing me so hard, I squeal. I savor each wanton pull, yank, and molesting of my body because it only serves to show me their passion, which I love.

I'm overcome with a desire to be fucked by Juan while Sebastian fucks him in the ass, the three of us lined up, all that thrusting, pumping, moaning, with all those man groans, would drive me to orgasm after orgasm. I'm yearning to hear the soft squish of dicks entering wet fleshy holes.

"Dammit, I'm so fucking hot," I murmur in a slightly slurred moan-like voice. "Juan, I need that cock in my pussy. Please. I'm begging you."

He nods and, without a word, but with intense lust-filled fuck-me eyes, he presses his fingers into my pussy to test me.

"Oh, I'm wet as fuck. I'm ready. Give me that cock. Fuck my cunt," I say in a commanding voice.

He obeys. Sebastian tugs my swim bottoms down and they cling to my knees. Juan presses the bulbous head of his cock, which is noticeably wider than his shaft, into my hot, wet pink core.

I groan out as does. He is so exquisitely manly that I melt against Sebastian. He holds me up as my legs start to give out. I sigh. I'm super happy we already have their condoms on because this fuck session is stoked, on high power to non-stop pound town.

"Fuck her hard, Juan. She likes her clit slammed," Sebastian instructs as he fully braces me from behind. I reach up and stroke his strong jawline.

Juan responds with wild, hard slams into my body and I almost scream, the pleasure is so overwhelming. I'm shoved into near euphoria as Sebastian stabilizes me against his body and plays with my nipples at once. This combination of multiple points of stimulation is what makes me come the fastest. I thrash and moan as my body skyrockets into the orgasmic plane where I'm so taken, I can't breathe. My body stiffens as I enter the peak of the orgasm. My mind is gasping for understanding but it can't wrap itself around the intense pleasure. My vagina contracts on Juan's cock so many times I can't count them, then they blend together as I reach a static state at the top of the orgasm peak, where little jolts upward give me multiple spikes. I gasp as the orgasm starts to wind down.

Juan quickly removes his cock from my body, most likely to save his erection from my boner demolishing squeezes. He surely would have come with the force my pussy was enforcing on him if he had stayed inside me.

"Wow," he mutters as he takes a step back, his arms raised in the air at the level of his chest. He staggers a bit and almost falls, but regains control. "Holy fuck! You are strong in the ways of pussy."

"I know, right? She's got an anaconda for a pussy." Sebastian kisses the air towards me. "I've heard her pussy rear down on a sex toy and stop the motor of it. It was fucking awesome as fuck!"

I laugh. "It's likely all the sex toy usage."

"Well, it fucking kicks ass!" Juan says as he steps back close to us.

"Mmmm, that was epic. I loved being between you two. Maybe, well, maybe we could all do doggy now." I glance at Sebastian to assess his willingness to actually fuck Juan in the ass.

Juan puts his hands together and takes turns making eye contact with me and Sebastian. "I love a good stimulating cock on my prostate. Will you?" he asks while holding Sebastian's gaze.

"I'll try. I've never done it," Sebastian says, finally sounding like he's interested in being intimate with Juan too.

"It's just like fucking a pussy, my dear man. Enter slowly and thrust on repeat. Follow the moans is your lotion for the motion." His slogan fits his personality to a T. Juan turns his ass towards Sebastian and motions for me to come around. "Come, Ruan."

I am shaking with excitement. I'm so wishing I could see Sebastian's face during this. Will we be shocked later that we did this? Honestly, I don't care. Our time together is about fulfilling each other's fantasies, and this is one of mine. I smile. I'm so pleased Sebastian is open to trying this finally. He can punish me later if he so chooses. I might get off on that, as likely might he.

I grip the chair in front of me for support as I lean over. Juan's hands are on my hips as he presses his cock at my entrance. One of his hands leaves my hips and guides his cock inside my pussy. His cock feels just as amazing the second time around.

I moan as Juan speeds up his thrusts, but then slows. I imagine Sebastian must be entering Juan's butt. Juan groans out loudly and then returns to thrusting into me. Knowing that Sebastian is setting the thrusts for the three of us is intoxicating. It's like he's the one in control of both Juan and me. Juan pounds me voraciously and Sebastian's grunts send twitches through my clit.

"Oh, my, gawd," I say through pants. "Fuck, fuck, fuck!"

Juan rides me, and Sebastian rides him for a few minutes. Even though the music is loud, the skin smacks are audible, the wet skin unmistakable, and the moans and grunts of all of us blend in the air. We are a fucking symphony.

"Oh, fuck," Juan says, followed by, "Oh fuck, yes." Then a giant groan that sounds like he must be coming.

I moan as I am slammed into my orgasm and Sebastian yells out next.

Juan still slowly pumps his cock into me as I float down from the apex of my climax, I savor the satisfied sighs of the two men.

Juan pulls out of my vagina and rubs my hip. "Epic fuck," he says. "Thank you, my man, Sebastian. You got my prostate good. Whew!"

Sebastian chuckles. "I did okay?" He glances at Juan, then quickly averts his eyes to his cock to remove the condom.

"You did killer, my man. Absolutely a natural."

I snicker. "I wish I could have watched that."

"That was one of the most erotic sex scenes I've ever witnessed live. Well done." It's a new voice, a male one. "Sorry, I didn't mean to watch uninvited, but I'm getting slammed out there, Juan. I need you." The bartender claps his hands together. "But damn good show, you guys. Better than porn, and I'll be replaying that in my head on repeat."

Juan laughs. "One of the best, huh?" He peels his condom off.

"You outdid yourself this time, Juan."

"Well, it's thanks to them. They invited me."

"Jealous, just saying, I'm jealous. But good on you all." He claps Sebastian on the back. "Drinks are flowing my friends, I bet after that, you could use a refreshment."

"Oh, most definitely," I say. "Thank you, Juan. That was a fantasy of mine and I really appreciate you being a willing part of it."

"Oh, my pleasure, Ruan. Sebastian. A right good fuck I won't ever forget."

I straighten up my swimsuit as Juan and Sebastian dress. "Need an orgy catamaran cruise."

Sebastian chuckles. "Don't laugh. They exist. You just need to know the right people."

"Wow, I might have a new fantasy brewing."

Juan waves and follows the bartender toward the bar.

Sebastian pulls me into his arms. We share a peck.

"Did you enjoy that, Ruan?" he asks.

"I did. Very much so. Thank you for being open to it."

"Well, the alcohol helped that, but it wasn't as terrible as I thought it might be. I mean, I came, right?"

"Right! Exactly. As did I. Wow. This was unforgettable. An epic one for the books."

"Can't argue with that."

He takes my hand, and we return to the party. We exchange knowing happy glances with Juan for the rest of the cruise and hug him as we disembark.

Chapter Eight
Sebastian

Back at the beach house, Ruan and I are relaxing in the hammocks under the deck, dozing. The waves cooperate and sing their soul-soothing song. The wind is turned to a low whisper. I watch couples walk by, some with dogs, some with kids, and one group of five women talking excitedly. The beach walking entourage doesn't slow one bit the whole time we lounge. Once I spy Ruan stirring, my heart leaps.

"Babe, you waking up?"

She makes that sweet sound she does when she stretches in the mornings as her arms shoot out straight and she twists her body in the hammock. Her bikini top has shifted so that both nipples are delectably exposed. The familiar first rush of blood surges through my cock and it jumps to the right inside my suit. As it fills more, it shifts more to the center. She looks absolutely delicious. I glance at my swollen cock pressing out the fabric. Down, boy. We need to wait until the sex swing is up. We've got work to do first.

"Yeah," she murmurs sleepily. "Damn, did I need that nap."

"Oh, me too. I didn't sleep long, but it was so refreshing."

She sighs, then gasps, then laughs. "Omigod, we really did do that today, didn't we?"

"We sure as fuck did, babe. I'm a bit overwhelmed by it too, but I'm so glad it was with you. I've never done such a thing before, truth be told."

"Well, neither have I. I've done some crazy things in my youth, but not quite like today. We will remember today forever."

"And it's not over. I'm fixing to set up that sex swing for tonight. You in?" I twerk my cock in my suit, it's so hard and it feels bigger. Blue balls now will be worth it fucking Ruan in that swing later. "I'm thinking, why not leave it up for whenever we want to slip you into it and fuck?"

"I'm in," she blurts as she glances at her chest. "Oops. It's like sleeping in a tank top, they never stay inside." She chuckles and starts to fix it.

"Please don't. You look so sexy and beautiful."

She smiles and a wave of pleasure rides her face, which pleases me immensely. I love complimenting her, making her feel sexy. "You were so generous today. You realize how sexy that is? What you did was epic."

"I actually enjoyed it. Can't say I'll ever seek man ass out again, but it wasn't as horrible as I had always thought it would be. But it definitely took me being drunk to try that."

"Yeah, my inhibitions were just gone." She runs a hand through her hair. "Oh. Ouch. Major beach wave tangles. It's like old raggedly doll hair right now."

"Now that's gonna be great for grabbing your hair from behind with later. More grip."

She drops her mouth open wide. "What? Oh wow. I hadn't thought of that, but you are right. I'll wait to shower then, give you something to hold on to." She snickers. "That's a pretty hot thought."

"Indeed. It's a bit like dreadlocks." I sigh and resist the urge to stroke my cock. "So, do we have a plan for dinner or are we ordering in?"

"I have steaks if we want to grill. They can be grilled tonight or tomorrow, but tomorrow at the latest."

"Okay. I'm up for grilling." I rub my hands together. "I've got mad chef master skills, as you know, with steaks."

"Yeah. You do. And I'll make a salad. Sautee some mushrooms, zucchini, and onions in butter. I make this amazing balsamic drizzle.

Then I have that loaf of French bread we can butter. Pop open another bottle of red. Whew! We are certainly lushes today!"

"No doubt. But a glass or two with dinner won't make us drunk, just feeling good."

"Agreed." She slips out of the hammock, leaving her nipples still exposed, and we walk up the deck stairs. I grab at her butt as she takes the steps, and she squeals with each pinch.

"Oh, damn, if I hadn't planned the swing, I'd savagely fuck you in the living room right fucking now. You are driving me wild." My cock throbs. I love the curve of her ass and hips.

"Maybe you should cover up, so I don't accidentally mount and fuck you." I laugh as we enter the house.

She cracks up. "Accidentally? Like your dick is so slick it just accidentally slips between my legs? Do I fall down and my legs swing up in the air in this scenario?" After her laughter subsides, she says, "Yeah, I'll get a coverup. No sense in dressing."

I can't not laugh with her when she laughs. "I like your reasoning," I tease.

She disappears into the bedroom, and I make my way to the garage to look for charcoal. When I return with a bag of charcoal and lighter fluid, she is dancing to music in the kitchen as she preps food. I love cooking with her, it makes me feel we are domestic in some way. It doesn't get more real than cooking, eating, and cleaning up together. The basics are sexy with her in their own right. Something I never thought of when I was younger, but is becoming more and more my feelings at twenty-six, almost twenty-seven. I've grown a lot over this past year, thanks to Ruan. With just over a year under our belts, my life has never been better, but it's more than that. I need her.

We exchange smiles as she bobs her head to the music. She does a little hip shake as she sings along. I almost trip over the couch side table looking back at her. She laughs as I make a silly face before turning around to walk, looking forward like a normal person. She's a delight.

Just need to get her to see we need more time together. That's the challenge.

The wind cooperates and our candle flame remains alive at the dinner table. It's not even dark, but Ruan lit the candle just to watch the flame flicker. Her eyes sparkle as she talks about the erotic romance novel she's currently writing. I could watch her talk about it all day with the way she lights up, the way she enjoys it. We sip red wine and enjoy juicy steak, a crisp salad, buttered bread, and the mind-blowingly delicious veggies with the balsamic drizzle.

"You really made up this recipe for the drizzle over the vegetables?"

She nods. "Yeah. I do enjoy cooking and making up recipes."

"It's unbelievable. I've never tasted anything like it."

"Well, you are used to microwave heated corn dogs and box mac and cheese, so ..."

I feign mock shock. "Hey, I cook more than that. Those are just meals when I'm in a hurry or exhausted. Plus, they are cheap. Cheap and fast. Pop open a can of soup, then I'm all good."

She chuckles. "I get that. Fast and cheap is good. I kind of want to use that as a book title." She guffaws it up. "Sounds hot, doesn't it?"

I join her in laughter. "I love your writer brain. It never stops, does it?"

"No, it doesn't. Which is why I love the notes app. I can capture thoughts at a moment's notice." She wraps her lips around the steak on her fork and it gives me great pleasure to watch. "Did you hear back from the car repair?"

"Yes, it will be ready tomorrow, but it can sit for a bit too. Four thousand dollars. I'm so thankful I have a deductible."

"Oh yeah, totally. That's a necessity. Car repairs suck and they always seem to just fall in your lap."

"Yeah. I'm never prepared for them. Even though I know they are a fact of life."

"We can go get it tomorrow. Maybe after the amusement park would be a good time. What time do they close?"

I check my phone. "Eight. We should be able to make that, I'd think."

"Yeah, definitely. If not, we can just get it the next day, I assume."

"It feels nice, like we are a real couple when we discuss these kinds of things." I smile at her.

She gives a sweet, yet fleeting, smile. "Yes, Sebastian. I agree." But the words don't reach her eyes.

I dismiss my negative thoughts because it's about swing time. I have all week to convince her we are a real couple, and I'm not giving up that easily.

She cleans up the dinner, insisting I am more useful in setting up the swing. She's not wrong. The glasses of wine and food have us both relaxed and ready for some fucking.

"Brownies later," she calls from the kitchen. "Chocolate after sex is the best!"

"Agreed," I call back.

The swing is easy enough to set up with the ladder from the garage, it's just a clip of the D ring to the eye bolt. Easy peasy. She had widened her eyes when I sauntered to the sliding door, swing in hand. With three eye bolts hanging from the ceiling in this place, the one in front of the ocean is the most appealing. We'll use the kitchen and bedroom ones another day. I love surprising her. And I can't wait to spring my surprise on her. I'm thinking I'll wait a day or two more to get her anticipation to max point where she's ready to really explode from curiosity. Her begging is so sweet and delicious. The dominant in me just wants more.

"I've got it all set up. It just needs your hot little body slung into it."

She does a skip and jump, then claps her hands. "I can't wait to try out this swing!"

She scampers off to the bedroom and I watch her from the couch, holding my cock at the base and shaking it like a cane.

"I'm ready," I call after her. I have no clue what she could be doing, but I know I'm going to like it no matter what.

She bounds out of the room with an armful of sex toys. "I'll get the whole arsenal so you can pick and choose, if you want. We don't need to use any at all. You are in charge." She grins seductively. "Bend me, mold me, swing-fuck me. I'm all yours."

"Music to my ears." I spy several rabbit sex toys, a few clit suckers, a large flesh-colored dildo, a blindfold, a spanking paddle, and a magenta curvy squiggle wand.

"You get to pick what we do. I want you too."

My heart skips a beat as my lust rages. Her demure declaration giving me control is exactly what I've always dreamt of from a woman. We fit together so well, it's almost ridiculous. This is my dream come true. Ruan in a sex swing overlooking the ocean, with a pile of sex toys to satiate my lust, and hers, every sexual whim.

"Get over here, Mommy," I say. "Your boy needs to get that juicy ass."

She skitters over, dancing about with glee.

'A joyful woman is a blessing', my dad always used to say. My mom had been playful, just like Ruan. It used to make me cringe to watch my parents at times, but now I see what a gift their example really was, and I'm grateful. Wait, shit, no parent thoughts right now. I shake my head to shove off the images and focus my gaze intently on Ruan. She still has the coverup on over her swimsuit.

"Let's get you strapped into this thing. I'm thinking it may be a challenge at first, but I'm betting we can shave down the learning curve real quick." I pull her to me close, her body on mine arouses me even more. I'm pretty riled up; I'm going to need to do a lot of pulling out to get her to come first. But I'm up for the challenge, stoked for it really.

We kiss and grope each other, our lust proving more and more ardent by the second. Her kisses are hungry. I match them as we make out on the plush couch.

I stand and pull her up as well. We kiss again and I cup her ass with a firm grab with both hands, which makes her flinch.

"Oh," she mutters. "Mm. Love your hands on me."

I remove her coverup and swimsuit, tossing them across the room as she chortles with delight.

She looks over at the swing. She looks nervous, but excited. I scoop her up and carry her to the purple and black mini hammock. Having the door open gives us a nice light breeze, the sigh of the sea brushes us through the open door. I gently lay her on her back in the scoop of the swing and secure the straps. I swing her about and compare her level to my cock to see if this will work.

"You are a little too low. Let's get you back out and I'll adjust it."

I help her out of it, and she stands beside me, watching me make the adjustments.

"I'm sure glad you are handy. I'm not sure I could figure this out. It's definitely not my forte."

"Ah, this is easy for me, actually." I help her back into the swing and maneuver her toward my body. "Now that's just right."

I adore her pleased facial expression.

She blows a puff of air to fluff a curl away from her face. She can't do it, so I hook the lock of hair behind her ear. "Thank you. The owners of this place sure knew what the fuck they were doing."

"Yeah, the eye bolt in the block of wood is genius. This place is literally perfect for us. Perfect location. Perfect size. Sex toy hardware included."

"Yeah, and, when I saw the eye bolts in the description of the house, that alone would have sold me, but then everything else was just perfect too."

I give her an intense stare. "Right?"

I push her in the swing, and she laughs with delight as I spin her around.

"Wee," she squeals. "This is really fun."

"And I'm not even fucking you yet." I grin a devilish grin.

I fondle her shapely shins, savoring touching her body as I make my way up her legs, fondling and kissing, licking, nibbling. Each nibble she gasps, or squeals, or sighs. Just utterly fun. I adore how I can maneuver her body so easily in any direction within the full 360-degree span.

"This is sheer genius!" I exclaim as I swivel her sideways to the oceanfront.

"And it's as comfortable as the reviewer said it would be, which is a huge relief. So many designs said the straps cut into the skin after a while or gave bruises."

"This is an ideal design," I speak breathlessly into the skin of her thigh.

She shudders, which excites me further.

As I come nearer and nearer to her pussy, her breathing becomes more labored, as does mine. I don't hesitate but slide my tongue along her slit. I maneuver my tongue all over her lips, pulling each one into my mouth and suckling before I move on to flick her bean. Over and over again I run the tip of my tongue across her clitoral glans. She cries out with each firm caress. I can't get enough of her fleshy folds against my tongue and lips. I press my fingers in, working her into a frenzy with both my tongue and fingers. Her increased moaning tells me she's loving my strokes.

Scanning my sexual move toolbox in my head, it's time for the aggressive moves. I charge in for a full hard suck of her whole external clitoral area and she screeches out her pleasure. I insert my index and middle fingers and find the right spot to squeeze her internal clit, pressing my fingers upward towards my mouth. She shrieks out and I smile while still in deep suction of her clitoral head area. I've learned to not lose that suction so she can climax hugely, such a reward as a man to make her come hard.

She struggles and writhes; she can't touch me because she is strapped in. She tries to reach me, her failed attempts turn me on. I'm in control, she's losing it, which is perfect for the budding Dom in me. She grunts and her sounds are almost pouty. I'm loving the power this sex swing gifts me as she sounds more and more edged, and desperate, with each second.

I stand and tap my hard cock on her clit up and down her lips in a zigzagging pattern, rubbing her lips and parting them with my cockhead on repeat, using my cock as I would a sex toy. If I'm honest, this feeds my ego, which feeds my libido. I'm going to fuck her silly.

Her moans are growing insistent, which is so hot.

"Please, put your cock in me, Sebastian. I need it." Her sweet sexy voice getting whiny is just what I want.

"Beg me. Beg me to fuck you, Ruan. Beg me to fuck you hard."

I repeat the whole entire tapping cock play along her slit as her moans get more and more wanton. I'm loving this! I plunge my cock tip in for a taste of her wet pussy. We both groan out. I thrust into her but pull out again to tap her clit more. She gasps and moans so out of control I can't help but smile. I never knew how delicious a sex swing could be.

I dip my cock in her again for several pumps.

"Yes, yes, yes, fuck me, Sebastian. Please, I need you to fuck me hard. Please."

I agree. Her helpless pleading lights a trigger in me and I'm more than ready for this rage fuck. I slip inside her smooth hole and aggressively ride her pussy non-stop. Her moans elevate quickly to the point I can tell she's about to climax. I've got her so aroused to the perfect spot that it won't take much clit play and thrusting to push her right over that orgasm edge. But I change my mind at the last second, I pull out and bend over to suck her clit hard, my fingers digging into the soft flesh of her thighs.

Her yells ramp up so loud I imagine if anyone is walking along our shore, they will hear her shouts. Her body curls and twitches, and she loses her breath, something I often strive for when fucking her. Her torso twitches forward, the sling cooperates and follows her body lurch forward. Her legs go stiff, and her toes curl. Fucking perfection.

I suck her harder as she gasps for air as her body travels the course of the orgasm. Slowly, her breathing wanes to slow sighs. I continue to suckle along her slit to ensure she's fully finished her climax. I heartily fish my tongue into her to scoop all her cum, which is sweet, but salty, and musky. I smear the thick fluid all around my mouth with my tongue to savor her sticky spill on every tastebud.

"Mmm," I moan as I devour her ejaculate down my gullet. "Mmm. Give me it all, babe. I want it." I puff my panting right against her wet hole.

Her breathing is still labored, but the look on her face is satisfied. Exactly where I want her to be.

I unstrap her and say, "Tummy down, mommy. I'm gonna slam into your buttocks. Fuck you so hard you can't breathe." My expression grows evil. Yeah, I'm going to slam her ass with multiple things.

I lift her up and help her to flip over.

"I going to fuck you doggy, right into the sky."

A shiver visibly runs through her body. She says breathlessly between pants, "Oh, this will be thrilling." She pauses as she tries to get comfortable in the sling. "I love the idea of looking out over the ocean as you doggy fuck me." She finally stops moving as she settles in.

I shift her a bit. "Are you comfortable?"

"Yes, I am." She sighs and it's scrumptious. It feeds me. "I already feel incredible after that last orgasm."

"Well, hang on, I'm nowhere even close to being done with you." I lean over her and whisper adamantly in her ear. "You're mine."

"Mmm," she says sweetly. "I love those words."

With her body in front of me totally vulnerable, her limbs hanging slack, her pert ass slightly presented upwards for me at the perfect angle, my masculine energy rages into a max desire to dominate her.

"I think we need a little punishment, mommy. Some payback. You made your stepson fuck another man today. That's got to be ... dealt with...punished."

She gasps, which is almost funny, she's the one who brought the paddle out. But then, I remember, role play. She's just playing her role. I'm enjoying mine already.

"Punishment?" she asks innocently, clearly playing along. "Whatever do you mean, son?"

I pick up the paddle and raise it above her perfect white creamy butt. I stifle a chuckle at the words 'Naughty Ruan' on one side of the paddle, and 'Good Girl Ruan' on the other side. "You coerced me into fucking a man in the asshole, something I never thought I'd do. You got me drunk." I slam the paddle against her cheeks at a moderate level of hardness. "I see you've done some painting work on here, mommy. Good mommy." I flip the paddle to the 'Good Girl Ruan' side and smack her butt with it.

She arches her back and cries out. "Oh, fuck!"

I slap her butt again with the paddle.

"And you took advantage of my lust to please you, mommy." Smack. The harder hit makes the swing lurch forward. Setting her body in exaggerated motion rages my dominance urges further and I smack her butt harder with the paddle.

"Oh, gawd damn!" she mutters.

"You need to take your punishment like a good little bitch, mommy."

I plow the paddle against her smooth reddening skin again. I take a step back and draw in a slow, deep breath to remind myself not to go too far like I did in Colorado.

"What do you say to your stepson for your sin, mommy?"

I slap the wood to her bottom once more. Hard.

"Oh!" she exclaims as she rides the trajectory of the swing that my spank set in motion.

I catch the swing to stabilize it. "What do you say to me?"

"I'm sorry," she says, then gasps deeply.

I gently paddle her buns with the paddle. "Good Girl." I set the paddle down because her ass skin is red enough. I tap my hard cock on her reddened skin. "Spank you with my cock," I mutter.

She shudders and groans. "Oh, fuck yes"

I press my cock along her ass crack and on to stroke her vulva lips. My precum mixes with her juices. We are ready.

I press my cock into her.

Chapter Nine
Ruan

As Sebastian begins slow thrusts into me, I rise up in the swing easily with each pump. While he has my hips secured in his hands, I am weightless in sheer comfort as he pounds into me because of the swing. It's exhilarating! With each slam he exerts against my ass, I glide towards the sky like I'm fluid, especially when he loosens his grip for a moment before gravity delivers me back to him.

When he ramps up his thrusts into me to a fast pace, I watch the clouds as I'm soaring up. The sensation that I'm flying above the sea floods my senses. I'm riding air as he projects me along with ramming his cock into me.

I stretch my arms up and towards the sea. "I'm flying," I shout.

Sebastian chuckles and fucks me harder, so I bounce off his body on repeat, each slam in more delicious than the next.

"Oh, fuck yes, this is hot," he mutters, then releases a deep yummy man growl that intensifies my edging. It shoves me along the climb up to the peak of my climax where I stay perched on the edge, waiting for my chance to come.

The waves crash forward as he pumps his abdomen against my butt, pushing me closer to the waves with each movement. Our fucking becomes ethereal, graceful, yet full of such force that my body is charging head-on into the peak of my orgasm. When he pushes me forward, I reach for the ocean and sync my energy with its mighty force. It's a soft dream that fills every awake cell of my body with graceful pleasure, a gift I will cherish for life.

The climax stalks me like a reaper. I whimper, then cry out, my voice joining the swishing of the beach wind, the soft roar of the ocean's waves as I approach the apex of the orgasm hard. So hard I'm actually fearful.

"Come for me, babe," he commands.

Music to me. With a sigh of relief, I give in. I allow myself to plunge into the full force my powerful clit sends across my body. My vagina contracts around his cock, sending sensations of pleasure all out across my body. He holds the swing still and groans as my vaginal muscles squeeze his erection inside me. I scream out without dampening my sounds. I yell out until I lose my breath as I fall silent as the waves of yum finish traveling my body. Then I gasp deeply.

He releases a deep, guttural groan as his cock pumps me full of his cum. He pumps his cock into me as my contractions milk it all into me. I notice the instant increase in wetness. He lightly grinds and thrusts in and out of me, efficiently mixing our cum in my honey pot. My pussy is downright sloshy now. He falls forward onto my back, but only partially lays his weight on me. We both remain still, breathing heavily as the roar of the waves floods our ears. Having his body all along the back of me is comforting and I'm safe, cradled, home.

I attempt to speak, but it comes out only as a whisper. "Wow. Just wow." I fall silent again for a bit because saying more is too difficult at this point. "Oh, fuck," I say while panting. "That was just ... utter bliss. It was unbelievable!"

He's still breathing heavily against my back with his cheek pressed to my skin, his body so warm on my back as my front is bathed in ocean breeze.

His voice is raspy. "Oh, fuck yes, it was. Wow is right. I never would have guessed it would be quite that epic."

"It was pure magic," I say, trying to regain control over my breathing but failing miserably, I'm still so worked up. "That was the best fuck of my life."

"Same, babe. That was mind-blowing."

I release a heavy sigh and it helps regulate my breathing back more to normal.

He rises to stand and presses his fingers to my thighs, then grips my ass cheeks and spreads them open. He lowers himself and falls, open mouth, onto my pussy lips, his tongue working over my lips, which I imagine must be puffy by now. He suckles along my slit, slurping and sucking, poking his tongue in to taste us together. Dipping his tongue down to my clit, he rides my swollen bean and full-on sucks my clit. Every so often the firmness of his nose grazes my flesh.

My body recoils away from the powerful suck he gives me, the swing allowing for a little give, but he pulls me back, claiming me. As he works his tongue on my engorged clit, I ride up my climax hill quickly and burst into another orgasm. He continues to suck, which forces me to cruise to another climax without ever returning to baseline. Then another. I am moaning and whimpering, gasping, and screaming out. I plow into yet another orgasm.

He comes off my clit and says into my pussy, "One more, babe, then I'll let you come down."

The puff of his words on my skin tantalizes my desire along its ascent once more. Though I'm totally overwhelmed and hardcore resisting the urge to twist away, I want him to push me further, just to see how far he can take me. "I want one more," I whisper. It's not a lie, but I'm scared of it.

He suctions his full mouth to my clit, his hands still spreading my ass cheeks wide. The orgasm swells in me. This is going to be a big climax. I yell out, unable to stop myself as I get lost in the intensity of the big orgasm. It wracks my body, raging through, destroying any semblance of calm like the powerful life force it is, and my body twitches its way through a quadruple peaked orgasm.

I remain still as my hot breaths fill the air, only breathing is possible. Shocked by the strength of it all, I lay still and silent. For now, I'm completely rendered useless, helpless, vulnerable. Just even thinking about it all is a challenge. Aftershocks keep claiming me, twitching through my clit and pussy lips like delicious little lightning bolts. Finally, after an eternity, I regain enough energy to sigh. And it's a big sigh.

"Good girl," he whispers into my pussy as he eats out the new cum my body has expelled.

"Wow. I mean wow wow wow wow," I mutter sleepily. "That was way beyond epic. Mmmm." Still coming down off elation, I remain melted and unmoving in the sling. "I'm going to need to write this one into a story. That was not only mind-blowing but, basically, mind-altering."

He laughs and squeezes my thighs. "Well, it was for me too. Leading you through that made me so happy. And I agree. Was easily the best fuck of my life. And I'm so excited it was with you, Ruan." He rises. "Let's get you out of this contraption and snuggle on the deck so we can listen to the waves."

"Perfect. Let's grab a blanket in case we need it."

"Good idea." He helps me stand, but I'm a bit wobbly. "You're a wet noodle."

"Yeah, big orgasms will do that to a girl."

"No doubt, mommy." He clears his throat. "You know that was just role play earlier, right? I'm not really pissed at you for the ass fuck. I was drunk, but I did it. I take full ownership of that. I just wanted to play punish you."

"Oh, I know."

"I admit I was totally reluctant, but I didn't feel coerced. I was open to trying it, not sure I'll ever do it again, but I'm glad we did that together."

"Me too." I sigh and hug him. I look up into his soft eyes and he bathes me in the afterglow of his gaze. "We sure are fulfilling each other's fantasies again, aren't we? Pretty hardcore fulfilling."

"Fuck yeah, right we are. Damn good too." He squeezes my shoulders. "I didn't spank you too hard again, did I? I tried to hold back, control myself."

I laugh wildly. "That was control?"

He gasps. "Oh, damn. I went too far again?" He sighs. "I thought I did better this time."

"I'm just teasing. I'm fine. I may not be able to sit down, but ..."

His face falls into shock.

"Kidding."

"Phew, oh good. That's a relief." He sighs. "I just had this overwhelming feeling to completely dominate you into submission. It was like a mood came over me, but I could sense a bit more ability to control myself this time. I liked feeling more in control, though."

"Well, I love you controlling me," I scoff, trying not to reveal my surprise at that feeling. "Well, sexually, that is, not elsewhere."

"Oh, yeah, just in the bedroom, babe. You're in control everywhere else, and I'll follow your lead." A twinge of wistfulness flits across his face, then he points towards the deck. "Let's get to the snuggling. I'll get water bottles, you get a blanket and I'll meet you on the deck."

"Perfect plan," I say.

We separate and go about our tasks.

After I grab a blanket, I saunter onto the deck in my robe. Sebastian is already there lounging in a pair of pajama shorts, looking sexy as fuck.

"Nice robe, babe, even better cleavage." He pats the lounge chair between his knees.

I giggle and settle in between his legs. The air is warm, so I toss the blanket to the empty chaise beside us. He hands me a water bottle, which I immediately open and chug half of.

"Wow, I was thirsty."

He snorts. "Orgasming that many times drained your body of fluids. A state I want you in everyday."

I laugh. "Oh my gosh, what a thought! I never really thought of it that way. Things to aspire to."

He snuggles me tightly with his arms and legs. He's a warm cocoon.

In a barely audible voice, he says, "We don't have to just aspire."

I sigh. "This is the life. I think I would be so happy living here on the ocean like this."

"Let's do it!" he exclaims.

Too late. I've opened a can of worms. Well, he was already there.

My silence prompts no further conversation. I don't dare speak.

Finally, he says, "Ruan, I'm serious about that. I'd live like this with you in a heartbeat."

I guess we are going there. "Sebastian, we've talked about this already. I don't want to revisit it."

"Well, maybe I do. I want you, Ruan. I don't need kids. I've said that from the start of our relationship. It's you who makes me so happy. Being with you again, it helps me realize I've never been happier in my life and I want this feeling for the rest of my life."

I sigh in exasperation. "Sebastian, I know we are having a wonderful time, as am I. Really, an unforgettable time. But this is just for now. We are having fun together. We are fulfilling each other's sexual fantasies. Let's love this time for what it is only."

"It's not just sexual fantasies for me. It's life fantasies. Being with you is my life fantasy."

"Yeah, and therein lies the issue." I hold my breath, wondering if this will be a mistake. "You haven't lived much life yet. You can't know what you want, and I'm not going to be the one to limit you. I care about you too much to ruin your life."

He guffaws. I've made him angry.

"I'm not a child, Ruan. I'm nearer to thirty than twenty. I know what makes me happy and I know what I want."

Shit. Now I've done it. I've talked down to him. I scramble to fix it. "But you said you don't 'need' kids. That doesn't mean you don't want them."

"Hey, if I had them, that'd be okay. But I'm happy with you. I want to be with you. I want this happiness to continue." He pauses. "I'm …"

I interrupt him. "But you are so young. You don't know yet. Being so young, you can't know. And I refuse to prevent you from experiencing those joys you could get with a younger woman." Now I'm not helping smooth things at all.

"Quit saying that! I know myself. You act like I'm a clueless teenager. I've lived life, and to assume I haven't is really quite insulting. I'm not some dumb childish buffoon just looking to get off, to fuck you and run. "

Fuck. I've got to nip this in the bud. We need a new topic right fucking now. I just can't go there with him. I give him a seductive smile as I stroke his thighs. "I'm excited about the amusement park tomorrow. I haven't been to one in years and years."

He's silent. Ugh. He knows what I'm doing. I can see it in his eyes. My heart sinks. I've really hurt him. But I need him to see us for what we really are, and that's just a fling. An affair. I'm not his marriage material.

I turn my face toward his bicep and plant kisses along it as I caress him. "I'm loving this time with you, Sebastian. I wouldn't trade it for anything in the world."

He releases a big sigh. "I am too. It means everything to me." There is a wavering in his voice that crushes my heart.

In a forced light-hearted voice, I ask, "Are you going to go on the biggest roller coaster with me? I'll likely scream." I pause to see if this prompts a mood lift in his demeanor. "I'll go braless so you can see me in a wet t-shirt on the water rides."

He groans.

I smile. That did it.

"Oh, fuck. Now, that I can't wait for. Fuck, how are you so damn sexy?" He wraps me up tight in all four of his limbs, crossing his ankles over the top of mine. "I am imagining that right now. Feel that?"

His cock is filling like a steel rod against my back.

Relief floods me. I've successfully gotten us past the touchy subject of us and onto our fun.

"Well, fuck. I don't think you and I will ever be satiated. I'd fuck you right now too."

He blows out a puff of air over the top of my head. "I'm really enjoying sitting here with you watching the waves, though."

The moon is bright and shines off the tips of the waves as they come onto the shore while the rest of the sea is black. The rush of the wind picks up and whips my hair all about. He tucks it behind my ears, which makes me smile. He reaches for the blanket and covers us up.

#

I wake up to raindrops falling on my face.

"Oh!" I exclaim. "It's raining. Eek!" I scramble up off the lounge chair as the rainfall turns torrential.

He follows me as we rush into the house. We had left the door open, so the carpet was getting wet. Sebastian quickly shuts the door.

"Whew! That was crazy!"

I drag the wet blanket behind me. "Yeah, that was like an instant dumping from the sky."

"Well, it is Florida." He shakes his head and his wet hair strands flop against his forehead. "And it will be done in no time. Short. Hard and intense. Then gone. Florida style."

I laugh. "True. Very true."

"Dang. I'm drenched just from those few seconds." He laughs heartily. "Time to strip!"

"Yeah."

We both drop our wet clothes to the floor.

Our gazes meet and the intensity of our lust erupts. We collide and kiss, hands all over each other's wet torsos, gliding along wet hair, our hands hungrily gripping and fondling dampened skin. The moon beams itself into the living room, lighting up every light-colored item, including our skin.

He scoops me up and carries me to the bedroom. He places me gently on the bed.

"Be right back."

Glee fills me. I wonder if he's getting his surprise.

My panting doesn't slow as he rushes back into the room with the swing in his hands. He drops it on the bed next to me with a grin.

"Be right back. Need the ladder."

I giggle as I finger my clit, then slip a finger inside my wet pussy. I moan as he thunders back through the doorway, banging the ladder on the door frame in his haste.

"Oops, shit!" He rushes in, clanging the ladder a few more times on walls and furniture before the length is all the way through the door.

I laugh at his clumsiness. "We might need to make repairs before we leave!"

"It'll be worth it." He plops the ladder under the eye bolt and unfolds it. "We'd just need three swings at the ready if we lived here."

I pop up off the bed and sneak up behind him. I press my body to his backside, and he freezes in place.

"Mmmm. What a delicious feeling this is."

I roam my hands to his cock and stroke him. His precum flows instantly and I spread it down his shaft.

"We might be addicted to sex."

He chortles. "Ya think?"

He leaves my grasp to climb the ladder and I pout.

"Damn. Want you back in my hands."

"In a minute, babe. I want this set up so we can go hog ass wild fucking in it."

"Hog ass wild fucking. Now there's romantic talk!" I chuckle.

"Damn straight. Gonna dirty talk you into a wet pussy. Going to fuck you in circles, swinging your body around in this swing like you're a pinata, begging for my shaft of a cock to beat the goodies out of your pussy."

"Oh wow! There's an image!"

"And then I'll eat your insides that spill out."

"Oh, please do. Damn!" My lust thickens.

He climbs back down, cock bobbing deliciously as he descends. Once on the ground, he folds the ladder and places it against the wall. "This ladder would make a good brace for you to hold on to as I fuck you from behind. We'll need to try that later." The look of intense lust in his eyes sends a jolt from my clit through my pelvis.

"Oh, fuck, that got me."

We grab for each other and kiss deeply, both of us panting.

I take a step back and he pulls me to him, his brash impatience a scrumptious sign of his passion. I groan as he presses his body to mine, his hard shaft smashed between our bodies.

He scoops me up and places me tummy down on the sling of the swing. I situate myself as his impatience gets the best of him and he's inserting his cock into my pussy. It slides in like a hot knife into a hot pie, and with as much of a delicious promise. We both groan out. He rides my pussy hard and fast, taking moments to brush his hand along my clit. I take over and ride my bean as he fucks me ferociously from behind, his thrusts an insistent barrage of force. He comes first with a yummy satisfying set of grunts, which prompts me to come.

Our fast and furious fuck is the perfect pill for sleepiness. He helps me out of the sling, and we fall into bed without even bothering to turn off the lamp.

Chapter Ten
Sebastian

Sebastian's Dream

"Can't we just live in the now and not worry about the future?" Her eyes are aghast, pleading. Then they fall vacant like the dead, as if a switch got flipped. She's in a flowing white dress, like a ghost.

"I like to think about a future with you." I reach for her, but my hands slip through her, gaining nothing. My hope plummets.

"You can't," she says as she drops her eyes to the sand.

I want her gaze back met with mine. "Please. Look at me, Ruan. Don't you understand I want a future with you? I just want you and only you."

"Well, we are just now. Time is almost up, Sebastian."

"Can we at least think about our next getaway again?"

She pauses, then nods. "Yes. I can do that. Even if it's only a dream, my dear."

She doesn't even say goodbye, but walks away from me and no matter how fast I run. I can't catch up with her. She disappears into the sunset as if she herself is just a ray of light.

I startle awake with a gasp. Panic floods me until I spy her in bed next to me, breathing like she's still asleep. My heart is racing, my brain is confused. The feeling of losing her is so fresh from the dream. I can't shake the horror I felt when she walked away from me and I couldn't reach her. Logically, I know it was just a dream. But it felt real.

I slow my breathing to help me calm down. Fuck. Why is this so tough? It was a damn dream, Sebastian. I know she wants kids for me. A life with a wife my age. But what she doesn't seem to realize is that I'm in love with her. I audibly gasp. I'm jarred in place. That's real. Honest to fucking real. I'm in love with her. My eyes widen and an area of my aura expands, opens up, as if a veil has been removed. My new reality consumes me and I'm so happy. I close my eyes and pray for sleep.

#

The morning sun highlights a strip of skin along Ruan's side and up a sliver of her right breast. Having fallen asleep while spooning after that wild fuck had been so satisfying, despite my nightmare. Thankfully, the taste of the bitter dream no longer sours me as I gaze upon my beautiful woman. Her hair is spilled about the pillow in a fan. I brush it lightly with my fingers against the maroon pillowcase, her blonde locks a gorgeous contrast. I stare at her for a few minutes, memorizing this gorgeous image of her sleeping. I can do this. I can live in the now. My heart swells, and that familiar feeling I keep ignoring blossoms once again like a lighthouse beacon. I can ignore it, but its brightness is starting to blind me in each moment. I don't think I can live without this woman in my life every day. I'm tempted to say it out loud, so she hears it subliminally as she sleeps. Maybe that will help convince her on a subconscious level, so a bubbling up of realizing happens with time. I stroke her cheek and she stirs.

"Good morning, beautiful." I run my hand down her cheek on repeat. "How did you sleep?"

"Mmmm. I slept so good after that epic fuck. Wow. That was really intense."

"It was. I fucking loved it. A middle of the night fuck should be just like that, and just as rabid." I'm not even going to tell her about my dream. She might just agree with it.

"Agreed. Made me sleep like a baby. Probably a good thing with all the walking we will be doing today." She glances at the clock. "Oh, dang. We should get up if we want to get in line before they open. I know those entrance lines just get worse as the day goes on."

"Yeah. And the ride lines. I'm all for it. Let's get up, grab breakfast quick, and head out."

She runs through the shower as I start the coffee and spread the cream cheese on our croissants. We eat quick, then I shower as she applies makeup and we are out the door in twenty-five minutes flat.

The line to the entrance is already down to the parking lot from the entrance. We wait in line, the first of many, flirting and holding hands. We get a few looks, but mostly people are polite. I could care less. I'm happy and that's all that matters to me. Well, I want her happy too, but she's a bit more hesitant, but I'm aiming for changing that. There's no reason we can't be together. We are both single. We enjoy each other's company. We fuck like rabbits on steroids. We grant each other's wants, desires, and needs. I love her. What more can a man want?

I watch her watch some young kids squirreling around with a smile on her face, I'm sure remembering her own son at that age. Her own son is not far off from my age. She rarely talks about him, but when she does, her face lights up. I hope one day to meet him. Our being close in age is what prevents her from diving fully into our relationship. That's a hard fact I can't fix.

"When are you bringing out your surprise?" she shifts back and forth on her feet, her eyes are loaded with insistence. "I need to know. Why are you holding out on me?" She stomps her foot.

I laugh. "Just so I can see this side of you," I tease. "It's rather delicious."

"Hmpf," she says, releasing a puff of air. "Not even a clue yet? I'm dying to know! And I've been waiting long enough."

I smile a devilish smile. "Okay. You're right. I'll give you a hint. It's three pieces."

"What? That's a lame hint." She pouts.

"Okay. It's leather. Custom made. I bought it online." I hold my breath and watch her face for any inkling of ideas.

"Hmmm. Leather. Three pieces. Well. Geez. A lot of things fit that."

I rub my hands together as we stop moving in the line for a moment. "This is going to be fun to drag this out all day."

She purses her lips. "It could be clothing, a harness, a body suit. It could be a crop. Or restraints." She pauses and nods, points at my face. "It's a spanking slapper. Or one of those pussy slappers." She cringes as she realizes how loud she said it as a woman nearby cringes and frowns, while the man next to the prudish woman smiles and chuckles.

"Kids here," the woman mutters with a haughty look.

"Yeah, so sorry," Ruan says as her cheeks blush. "Oops." She shrugs. "My bad."

Two teen boys behind us snicker and I shoot them a look. They shut up really quick, but Ruan looks amused, so no harm done. I turn back to the boys and wink. They visibly relax. Their looks of lust return. I smile, recalling the constant boners of being a teen boy, and how the mere mention of the word pussy elicited a full-body reaction.

The day progresses. We have an absolute blast. We ride all the roller coasters, eat all the junk food, and then some, and enjoy the shows. We eat our way through the day until the evening, when we head to the Italian restaurant on site where we have reservations. We approach the building, and we walk through the aroma of the beautiful rose garden flanking both sides of the entrance. The string of lights above gives off a soft yellowish-white glow. Italian music descends upon our ears as we saunter along. The light breeze lifts Ruan's blond curls, dragging the tendrils along her creamy white skin. When we stop because of the line to get in, I caress the edges of her bare shoulder blades with both hands, her skin so soft. I bend my head over and kiss her warm body.

"It's like walking through magic," Ruan says with a pleasant smile, followed by a shimmy of her shoulders as I drop kisses all along her flesh. "Mmm. How lovely." She draws in a deep breath. "Smell those roses."

I lean in and whisper in her ear, "I'd rather smell your pussy. Up nice and close with the tip of my nose penetrating you, getting wet from your slit."

"Mmm, well fuck," she mutters as firecrackers burst in her eyes.

Our gazes connect. If we were alone, we'd be fucking in a second.

"Can I help the next one in line?" calls a young woman in a little black dress. Her lips are a nice swollen pucker of red which she generously spreads into a shapely smile. "Do you two have a reservation?"

"Yes. Under Ruan Willow."

The hostess checks the screen of the tablet, taps it, and then looks up. She nods. "Okay. Yep. Here you are. Please follow me."

She leads us through all the tablecloth-covered tables. The candlelight flickers on the silverware and the wine glasses on the table, it's brilliant shine a sharp contrast to the black cloth beneath. The place is packed with people, a light hum of voices fills the room along with the romantic orchestra music playing. We are fully underdressed for the elegant polish of the restaurant, but everyone is, being this is an amusement park.

The hostess spreads her hand over the table. "Have a seat you two. I hope you enjoy. Your waitress will be by shortly."

She sashays away and both Ruan and I watch her ass tick-tock along. "Whew. Wouldn't mind bringing her into a fuck." Ruan smiles salaciously.

"No shit. She's hot as fuck." Not many women say that to their man. I'm lucky as fuck.

"I'd love to watch you fuck her while I suck her tits." She licks her pretty lips.

"Oh, damn. Now that's a damn good scene I'd love to get into." My cock thickens.

"You two would make gorgeous children."

She's smiling as I'm getting pissed. Did she have to go and ruin it? I remain silent as I try to not let my emotions rage.

"With both of your dark hair, both pouty lips, and deep, intense eyes."

The urge to spew hostility overcomes me. "Stop." I drop my eyes to the menu and bite down hard on the sharp replies I want to lash out with.

"Ah, come on, love, I'm just being honest. You will make a wonderful dad."

She won't stop pressing, so I blurt out, "That's so stupid, Ruan. I don't want that." This topic is now enough to make me vomit. I direct my angry gaze at her. "I've told you five hundred times that I want you." My voice comes out seething and I immediately regret it.

She widens her eyes as she lurches back in her seat. "Whoa." She fidgets in her seat. "I just think you don't realize ..."

I raise my head sharply to pierce her eyes with my outrage. But, for once, I'm going to shut up. I scramble for ideas to repair this mood we've fallen into. I take in a slow breath, then release it. I calmly say, "I'm going to order wine. Do you want red or white?"

She thinks for way too long before replying, "Red." She looks uncomfortable.

Fuck. The last thing I want to do is blow up at her and ruin our week together. But why does she insist on bringing this up over and over again ad nauseum? I reach for her hand and stroke it between mine, giving her my kindest eyes I can.

"I don't want to fight."

"Neither do I," she says indignantly. "Didn't think I was."

"I know." I smile at her. "I'll give you another clue about the sexy tool I brought along if you smile for me."

The corners of her mouth turn up. I sigh a huge sigh of relief when the smile reaches her lovely green eyes which, true to her chameleon irises, look more blue than green in the candlelight. "Tool?" asks with intrigue. "Okay. You win." She gives me a full smile.

"It will allow me to have a good handle on you."

"Well shit." The sparkling of her eyes flares brilliantly. "You've got me very intrigued. Is it something I wear?"

"Sorry. That's all the clues for now." I raise my left eyebrow at her seductively and place both palms flat on the table. "Fresh out of clues. I'm going to savor this tease as much as I can."

"You are a tease!" she exclaims. "A total tease. All day!"

It strokes my manhood that she's now aroused by the mystery, nothing better than turning a woman on. Especially a woman who I ...

The waitress appears, interrupting my thought. A thought I've felt for more than Ruan realizes. I so want to say it to her. Maybe, just maybe, that would change everything.

"What can I get you to drink?" she asks sweetly.

I smile back. "My lovely date and I would like a bottle of red. Cabernet Sauvignon. The Stone Market brand."

"Excellent choice." She nods and swivels quickly on her heels.

"Look at you for ordering." I fidget with my silverware wrapped in the linen napkin.

I smirk, though my instincts are screaming at me to rebel against her condescension. Keeping things light is important. I swallow hard as I try to reset my brain.

"What will you order to eat?"

Dinner flows well as we skate the surface of our relationship. Eating helps us have things to talk about, as does reminiscing about all the rides. But our differences are clearly the elephant in the room. After we pay, I drape my arm over her shoulders, her arm snugs my waist, and we saunter out into the warm sunshine of the evening. The light breeze picks up her shining strands of hair that she straightened for today. She took time this morning to straighten it, much to my chagrin, because

I love her curls. But, as always, she certainly looks stunning with her locks straight as well.

We walk along the water, the sun beaming as strongly off the water as it does from itself, and too many thoughts flood my brain.

"You know, I really am enjoying this week with you."

"Oh, Sebastian, as am I."

We exchange smiles before I decide to ruin it.

I stop walking and pull her to the railing along the water. I face her and she copies my stance. A big satisfied smile brushes across her face.

I'm ready to beat the dead horse. "When will you take us seriously, Ruan?"

Her smile vanishes. "I do, Sebastian."

"No, you don't."

I cringe as her face falls into a painful grimace.

"In fact, you treat me like a child."

She laughs. "Oh, sweet sexy hunk of man, you are certainly not a child." She raises her left eyebrow seductively, the look in her eyes an intense shade of lusty leering.

She leans closer to me and grabs my cock, which betrays the moment as it springs to life by hardening at her touch.

I resist the urge to step away from her. Closing my eyes, I do my best to wipe my face clear of anger. I'll table this for now. I want her enjoying our time together, but I'm not going to accept her views, I'm going to change them.

The look in her eyes flickers from deep want to a flash of worry, and back to lusty, so I follow suit and kiss her.

"Mmm," she murmurs as she fondles my erection through my shorts. "I think we need to go home so you can share what you brought here with me there."

"I can't argue with a horny woman. And why would I?" I give her a big grin as I migrate my hands to her ass cheeks. I give her buns a hearty squeeze.

She squeals and presses her generous breasts to my abdomen.

"I need to see those things bare and get those nipples in my mouth." I take a step away from her and grab her hand. "Let's get out of her before our groping disturbs the peace."

She nods. "With that thing in your pants all ready for me, I rather want to run out of here, but don't want to alarm people."

The drive home is all about edging. We can't keep our hands off of each other. She gives me road head topless as I drive. I almost crash as she giggles and wipes the cum from her lips. She presses her finger into her mouth to eat all my cum.

"Whew," I stammer. "Fuck! That was almost a disaster."

We carry on as if no one got pissed today, as if no one brought up our dilemma. I'm buying the denial she's selling, blissfully so.

"We could have just needed another car repair."

Her response is simply to giggle and give me fuck me looks. "That's for the rental place to deal with, should it happen."

I brusquely turn into the driveway of the beach house and come in hot. I slam on the brakes just prior to smacking into the garage door.

"Wow," she slurs. "Feeling rather aggressive, aren't you? That's perfect for our next stage of the evening."

"Yeah, my cock is still hard. I can't stop thinking about how you are going to look in about ten minutes."

We scamper into the house, me slapping her bottom as she shrieks. She's such a fucking delicious woman.

"Sit on the couch," I command as I point.

She plops her butt on the couch. "Yes, Daddy. Or is it Sir? Or what is it this time?"

I cock my head and pet my puckered lips with my forefinger for a few seconds. "I'd say this time, it's ... Master."

"Oh!" Her perfectly shaped lips stretch into an O. "Well, then. That's new."

"Sit tight, my pet." My cock throbs in my pants. "Don't move. I will undress you when I decide."

"Mm. Wow. I love this, Sebastian. I want you to dominate me. Make me your bitch."

"You already are my bitch. Now you are going to really feel it."

She licks her lips and kisses the air before I turn around and head to the bedroom. I dig in my suitcase for the red satin bag. The cinched bag sports a tag with the words 'My Pet Ruan'. My lust engorges as my cock fills a bit more. I almost run out of the room but force myself to take a deep breath so I can walk dignified, like a Master should. I am in control. I am in control. I am in control, I chant inside my head.

Her eyes widen with delight when she sees the red bag in my hands.

"Yay a present. Is it for me, or for you?"

"Both," I say firmly as I stand in front of her. "Take out my cock and suck me," I command, even though she just did that on the drive, but I couldn't have known she was going to do that. She obliges my direction and pulls my cock out. With both hands on my shaft, she inserts my cockhead into her hot, wet mouth without a single complaint that she just did this.

I groan as I fondle her hair and slightly pump my cock into her mouth. I reach down and give her left butt cheek a swat.

"Do better, bitch. Suck me hard."

She whimpers and with wide eyes she pumps her mouth up and down on my cock head, her hands spreading the skin on my shaft up and down vigorously.

I pull my penis out of her mouth and hand her the bag.

She claps her hands and bounces on the sofa, making her boobs jump nicely on her chest. She opens it and her eyes enlarge.

"Oh my," she says as she pulls out a black collar with fake diamond jewels and a matching leash, and a pile of red straps, all linked together in one unit. "Whoa. Holy shit, Sebastian."

Her facial expression slips between apprehension and wonderment. For the briefest moment, her lust is gone and a look of concern flickers.

"Oh shit," I mutter, when I meant to remain silent. "It's for you, my pet."

She gasps and sets the collar and leash aside so she can examine the strap garment. "Harness?" she asks with a slight grin.

I breathe a sigh of relief. "Yes. Now stand up. I'm going to strip you now."

She obeys with little mewling sounds that make my cock jump.

I remove her white top and immediately snake my tongue inside the top seam of her bra to taste the skin of her breast mound. She tastes slightly salty.

"Gotta taste you where no sunscreen is," I mutter rashly.

"Oh, I know, right? Dang sunscreen."

I fondle both her breasts as I continue to lick inside her bra. I reach around to her back and undo the clasps. The bra clings to her large orbs. I cup them and then slowly peel the bra away from her. Her breasts flop out, nipples so erect they look as if I've pinched them.

"Nice, fuck you have perfect breasts. Amazing nipples. And I know nipples." I suckle her nips, each one in turn as she fondles my hair.

I reach down and grab the collar and open it up. Her eyes do something funny when I press the collar to her throat. I hear her swallow as despair flicks across her eyes.

"Is this okay, Ruan?"

She nods but says nothing.

I secure it around her neck, not too tight, but snug. She doesn't say a safe word, so I continue.

I slip off her skirt to bare her pussy and ass. Her being commando all day has driven me wild. Being so close to her all day and in the heat, I could constantly smell her. It made me randy all damn day.

"I loved it when you fingered my pussy on the tunnel ride." Her voice quivers, like she's struggling with something.

"I wanted to do more."

I pick up the harness and spread it out so I can figure out best how to get it to hug her bodacious curves.

"You look fucking amazing," I say as I slip the red-strap garment over her head.

I snug all the straps in place.

"I left your pussy and ass bare on purpose, mind you, my pet."

"Yes, Master. Thank you."

She's an obedient role plaything. I snicker as I tug her towards me, using the strap across her left breast.

"See how I will have a handle on you?"

"You will have lots of handles on me, Master."

I click the leash into the ring on the back of her neck before I push her to the floor. She follows my hand directions and gets on all fours.

"Crawl to the bedroom, pet."

She obeys. As she crawls past the couch, I yank the leash, smack her ass to get her to go faster.

She pauses and gags.

I bite back my surprise and release the tension on the leash a bit.

I spank her butt again to get her moving again.

She continues to crawl, but stops as she gags again.

"Oh," she gasps, then releases a whine. She sits and looks up at me with pleading eyes. "I'm sorry. I don't think I can handle this. I'm fighting gagging every second. I won't be able to come with this thing on."

My throat drops to my heart. "Oh, Ruan. I'm sorry."

She raises a hand. "No. Wait. We can do it for you, but I won't be able to climax like this. But I want to do this for you. I want to give you this fantasy you obviously have."

I reach for the collar to remove it. She stops my hand.

"No. Leave it on. For now. Use me. Fuck me with it on, then can come my turn for pleasure. I want you to."

"I don't think I can come knowing this, Ruan." I kneel on the floor beside her. "It's okay. We don't have to do this. I don't need it. Just thought I'd try."

We both sit on the floor, gazing into each other's eyes, gauging if the moment is fully ruined.

Her eyes gain a burst of lust. "Honestly, you using me to get off is a turn-on. I want you to fuck me with this on." She touches my cheek. "Please. I want to give this to you."

I shake my head. "No. I can't do it. My cock has started to deflate." Turning her off is not a turn-on.

"I can handle it for a bit. Just do it. It may even get me off. Who knows? Maybe I'm wrong. Maybe I will come."

My mind flitters all around to the possible scenarios.

She sits on her knees. "Hey, think of it this way. We are exploring our boundaries together. I think I know how I will respond, but I could be wrong. I might be into it as we are doing it." She pauses as she trails her hand down my chest, tummy, and onto grabbing my waning erection.

Her touch brings my cock back to life instantly, and it fills.

"Are you sure?"

"Positive. Let's look at this as an experiment. I'll use the stoplight safe word plan."

I nod. "Okay. I'm interested in trying this if you are." Her trust in me means everything.

She repositions herself to being on all fours. "Take me, Master. Take your pet and fuck her."

I release a big sigh, which helps my tension dissipate. I pick up the leash and spank her ass again to get her moving.

She tries to hide another gag and a sick feeling floods my stomach.

"Ruan," I say with absolute hesitation.

"I'm telling you to proceed, Sebastian."

The harness is amazing on her body, almost highlighting her sexy curves. It's like it was custom made for her.

"You really look so sexy and amazing, my kitten." I almost bought cat ears or a catsuit, but the harness was just too incredible to pass up. The name does it all, we don't need ears.

She purrs as I lightly slap her ass with the leash. She stops at the edge of the bed and sits on her bottom, with her hands on the floor, like a cat would. Her grin and the look in her eyes are calm, yet I wonder what she's fighting to not show me.

I pat the bed and she jumps up.

"All fours, kitten."

My cock swings as I sway. I reach under her and play with her pussy, fondling her vulva lips, her slit, dipping my fingers inside her hot core to collect her internal sex juices. I drag my fingers along her slit to spread some of her wetness along her clit. I work my fingers in circles around her clit and press it hard to massage her arousal up even higher.

She moans and drops her head, which elicits a gag. "Fuck," she whispers. She recovers. "I'm okay. Fuck me, Master. Fuck me hard and raw. Use my pussy to come." She straightens out her spine. "I give you full permission to fuck me like this." She pauses. "In fact, I want you to."

Her asking me to do this is the only thing that's keeping my cock hard. I press my bare cock to her slit and rub it all over her opening to collect her precum and spread mine to join hers. I test her pussy with my fingers.

"You are very wet." I let some of my worry go because she's clearly aroused.

I press my swollen head into her pussy, and she moans out.

I groan as I slowly push the full length of my shaft into her womanhood. I begin to slowly pump myself into her, savoring every thrust, every rub where I get the honor of touching the most intimate areas of her body. I pull the leash slack up a little as I increase my speed of riding her hole with my hard dick. I ramp it up quickly to ram myself into her on repeat. Watching her tits swing back and forth in the harness almost takes me right over the edge, but I pull out for a few seconds to reclaim my control.

I aggressively shove my cock into her and pound her. My body slams against her ass cheeks making them gyrate back and forth. Dominating her rages my lust further and I yank on the leash.

Her head jerks back and she gags as I slam into her relentlessly. I take her pussy as mine and fuck her hard as she moans and gags. My masculine energy swells and I rail her without restraint.

She gags again and gasps out, "Yellow."

I stop thrusting immediately and pull out.

She swivels her head to look back at me, her eyes full of questions.

"It's red for me," I say with confidence.

She looks like she's about to protest but closes her mouth.

She swivels to sit on her bottom, and I sit next to her. I remove the collar and lay it on the bed.

"I was going to urge you to continue until I hit red. But then I realized, we both need to respect each other's safe word usage. You said it. I need to respect that too."

I smile at her as I pick up the collar. "I've got an idea to make this work for both of us."

Chapter Eleven
Ruan

Sebastian crawls behind me with the collar and leash in his hands. I eagerly yearn for his next move, my heart starting to race as the mystery swells my lust.

"I can own you in a different way. One that works not only for me but, most importantly, for you."

That sentence kneads my submission to right where it needs to be. Relief from having the collar off continues to flood me, that much I can admit.

He drags his fingers along my skin, kisses my shoulders. His touch gives me comfort, his breath on my flesh feeds my want.

"You are mine," he whispers with the hot puff of his words bathing my skin with each one further raging the fire in me, as an oxygen blow does to a flame.

I shudder and drop my head forward, his touch sending a jolt across my clitoris.

"I'm yours," I repeat. And I want it as much as he does.

He slightly lifts the metal circle of the harness off my back enough to slip the tip of the collar through it. I patiently wait as he clasps it. The straps radiate out from it like the spokes of a wheel. The straps spread down my back to the strap that encircles my waist. The other straps go over my shoulders, and the ones on my mid-back lay along my sides and wrap around, cupping my breasts like slender fingers. He gives the leash a practice tug. The harness and leash combo is like a web on me, giving him full control of my torso.

"Perfect." The satisfaction in his voice satiates my wish to please him.

He pulls it to guide me back on all fours, the modification proving itself instantly giving him full control of me to his will at any and every moment.

My pussy flares slightly with desire. "This is so hot," I whisper.

He strokes me from the top of my head to my ass in several long strokes, as one would stroke a dog or cat. "Good. Good. Good. That's what I want to hear from you, kitten."

He tugs gently on the leash, then increases the strength of his pulls. Each pull back forces my body to follow. The now smooth union of our sexual needs is intoxicating.

He man-growls and it rages up a deeper hunger inside me and all I want is him to rage fuck me again.

"Fuck me please, please, please," I plead. My voice comes out even more desperate than I thought it would. "Master. Please. I need it."

Our game is back on, and he commences fucking me from behind, with the level of aggression my true sexual appetite demands. Every so often, he exerts his domination of me further by jerking the leash. With his sounds, the act feeds him as much as it does me, and our fucking becomes a frenzied blur. I moan and cry out as he savagely fucks me hard, then harder and harder yet. The sounds of slapping from our bodies colliding in rapid succession is making me even hornier, wishing for more and more of him even though he's already in me. He's all-out pounding me like he's sexually starving. He abruptly stops, thrusting his thick manhood into me. He rides his fingers along my clit.

He pulls his cock out of me. "Wait. Don't move."

He leaves me and goes into the bathroom. As he comes out, I hear a buzz.

I smile. He's gotten my little bullet toy.

He hands the little buzzing toy to me and says, "Press this to your clit while I fuck you, kitten. I want to see if we can come at the same time."

I drop my upper body to the bed so I can press the vibrating toy to my clit. I moan out as I press it hard. He presses his cock back into me. It slides in so easily and we both react to him entering me with grateful groans.

He hardcore fucks me. He wrenches the leash every few minutes and grunts. I'm riding my climax hill banshee style, relishing the anarchy of this passionate fuck.

My body starts to tremble.

"Come for me, kitten. Come on my cock. Milk me."

He drops the leash on my back and grips my hips and nails me so hard. I curl towards the bed as I allow the orgasm to take me. My clitoris guides me into a giant orgasm, and I scream out, completely unable to stop my instinctual orations. The contractions start and I feel the circle of my vaginal muscles hug his hard shaft on repeat. I fall silent as I'm overwhelmed by pleasure.

He speeds up his thrusting, balls deep, and groans. "Fuck. Fuck. Fuck. Fuck."

His wetness spreads inside me as I twitch with aftershocks, my sighs filling the air.

He falls forward on my back.

"Wow," he whispers between pants.

"Wow," I parrot. "That was ..." I draw in a breath to appease my breathlessness.

"Epic."

We both sound totally satiated.

He rises and tips my hips towards the bed. I let myself crash down and then spread my body out flat. I scoot up so none of me is hanging off the bed. He does the same. We embrace. His skin is dewy with sweat and we both continue to pant. The scent of our sex fills my nose.

"How do we even keep topping the intensity? That was just ... almost indescribable." His words ring true.

"I know, you are right. We are such a match sexually that we just soar." My heart smiles.

"I know. I so wanted to continue. But I just couldn't. I couldn't not come after you did."

"I love when that happens, though. It's so sexy that you are overcome."

"I'm so happy we communicated and were honest, we would have never reached that high if we hadn't been honest with each other."

"That's so true. I see that now. And it helped me realize I need to respect what you are willing to do too. I don't know everything. Giving of myself has to work for both of us."

It feels like I'm talking about more than sex.

"Ruan. It meant a lot to me. And I want you to know I totally appreciated you trying and being willing to continue for me." He squeezes me and kisses the top of my head. "I've never had such a giving lover as you."

"You give to me every day, Sebastian."

"As do you."

We lay in bed in silence as our breathing slowly returning to normal.

"We are going to sleep so well tonight." I snuggle my body into his and soak in the post- glory of a damn good fuck. "Orgasms are great sleep aids."

"No doubt about that." He sighs.

I sigh.

"We should sleep," he says.

"Yes, we really should."

We are silent for a few minutes.

"Sebastian, I'm having an amazing week with you."

"I'm having an amazing week with you. It's better than I even expected, better than I dreamt it would be."

"Aww," I say, and my heart does that swelling thing that means more is happening than the rest of me realizes.

#

The next few days fly by as we play tourist by day, sex-crazed fiends by morning, afternoon, and night. We do it every chance we get, even once in the family bathroom at the mall. It's been sex beyond my wildest dreams. Our levels of daring, devotion, and obsessions with each other have far exceeded any and every potential stretch of my imagination. I honestly didn't think some of what we've done was even possible. I've certainly reached the biggest orgasmic and mental highs of my life. I'm already missing him by my side as our last full day looms against one of the best sunsets we've seen yet this week. The pinks and oranges flood the sky in their varying, majestic hues. The clouds cooperate as side drops as the sun's rays finger around them, highlighting their ethereal bumps, curves, and dips.

"What a beautiful night." Sebastian takes a sip from his beer. A sexy sneer overcomes his face. "Wanna set the alarm tomorrow morning and fuck on the beach as the sun rises?"

He let his stubble grow. I caress it, fingering the array of little strong bristly hairs.

"Yes, I love that idea."

"A good way to end our week together."

I instantly hate the word 'end'.

He eyes me up, his eyes scanning my face.

I lick my lips. After taking in a deep breath and slowly pressing it out, I say, "I'm sorry."

A look of shock floods his face. "For what?" he pipes up immediately.

"It's just all my own fears, and what I mean is ... not thinking of us as long term."

"Ruan," he begins, like he's about to lecture me.

"No. Hear me out. I need to say this." I unwrap myself from his arms and sit cross-legged in the lounge chair so I can face him. I owe him this. The constant roar of the waves calms me a bit. "I just don't want to want too much with you. It's been easier to just shove you off than to want too much of you. It's my way of putting up walls so I don't get disappointed. Hurt." I pause as I glance up at his eyes. His gaze is sweet, intent, loving, not gloating a single bit.

He touches my knee and rubs it. His eyes tell me more than anything.

I hold his gaze, as vulnerable as it feels. "It's just been easier for me to believe our relationship won't go beyond sex. Even right from the start, it's been easier for me to think of us as just a fling. You know the age gap role play fucking we love to do that rages us bright on fire, then simply burns out on its own? Then we move on to something else? I've thought of our whole relationship as being like that." I pause as I collect my thoughts. "I know you aren't a kid, Sebastian. You are a man. A full-grown, responsible, strong man. One I admire, so please know that how I've been acting is really no reflection on you. I just don't want to be your mistake. Something you end up regretting."

I want to pull my eyes from our mutual stare, but he swivels his legs so he can face me. So, I reposition myself so I'm fully facing him with my shins alongside his. I stave off the urge to burst into tears. It's not an easy feat, and I imagine he can read all of it in my eyes.

He takes my face in both his hands and plants a kiss on my lips. "You aren't my mistake. You are my purpose."

He says it with such conviction that I instantly feel full inside my heart. Full of him, full of us, and full of something I'm afraid to admit. My fear has all but dissipated.

"You have lived longer than me. True. You've had more experiences than me. Also, true. But you aren't living if you don't let us unfold into what we could become, Ruan." He squeezes my cheeks. "Take a chance on me. Believe in love and magic." He looks as if he's not done talking, but he says nothing more.

"You are right. I'm deciding we are done as we are growing, and that's not fair. No one knows the future. I shouldn't assume I do."

"Can we get a restart and begin this journey together afresh? Without making it just about sex? Without assuming we will fail and move on?"

"Well, I like sex." I allow myself to grin big.

He chuckles and releases my cheeks. "And I love that you do! I do too."

"I'm going to do better and not decide your life for you."

"And I'm going to be patient. Because I know I want you. I'm going to wait here in this mental space in our relationship until you believe that too."

I bite back tears as I let my heart feel that a little bit. It kind of hurts. My hope clenches inside me and I let it bloom, ever so little bit. But it feels amazing.

We beam smiles at each other as he pulls me over to snuggle with him in his lounge chair. I settle in and nuzzle my face against his chest. I want to touch him as much as I can before I can't.

Age is just a number that doesn't fit in our relationship. And it's high time I admit all of this. It was weak of me to dictate our relationship to mere triviality. I was just protecting myself but robbing us of the full score of each other. I can't call us done before we even get started. I've been a fool. Assumptions paved the way to the end of my marriage. I should most definitely know better than to assume I know another's heart.

"So, with all of that, I can assume our next getaway is solid, right?" His tone is more filled with slight joking than serious dread, as if he knows.

"Better fucking believe it. I'm on my way to having the image in my head already."

"How soon can we get a place booked?" There is joy in his voice that I want to pocket inside my heart.

"ASAP. I will book it immediately. Any requests? I was thinking like on a lake in the wilds of Canada or possibly near Niagara Falls. Some secluded cabin in the woods where we can make lots of noise fucking."

"Well, that sounds amazing. I've never been to either place, so I'm in. And if I can't swing a plane ticket, I'll drive." He straightens up. "Which reminds me. We need to get my car. We'd better get going so we don't have to squeeze it in tomorrow before your flight. I'd rather spend all day here with you, as much time as possible."

"Agreed. Let's go."

#

The wind whips my hair, stirring it all around my face like streamers on a stick as we drive with the windows down, singing to blasted music we can barely hear. Our heart-to-heart talks have me in such a good place I'm free as the wind playing with my hair, caressing my skin. I reach over and place my hand on top of Sebastian's, which is resting on the armrest as he drives one-handed. I am blessed beyond belief and here I am, pushing away a man who adores me, fucks me into blissful oblivion, and wants a future with me. I'd be a moron to fall into the poor me I'm old bucket. I smile as the elation fills every speck of me and radiates out.

"I'm loving this look on your face," he says with a smile.

"I'm feeling fabulous."

"Me too."

It's not too much to bask in glory after the week we've had.

He pulls into the ice cream shop parking lot and parks.

"We need ice cream before we get my car." His face is boyish and sweet, yet sexy, hunky manly.

"I love your thought process."

We get out of the car and the sun hits us like a brick.

"Whew! Hot one!" I exclaim, adjusting my sunglasses.

He grabs my hand, and we walk into the little shop.

Inside there are only a few people in line, so we snag a spot quick before someone else comes, not that we are in a hurry or anything. A woman with three kids in front of us struggles to keep them all calm and not screaming. I remember those days, though only having one I had it much easier. The fear of what Alex will think when he finds out about Sebastian tries to extend itself like a web in my brain. but I mentally shake it off. Not now. I'm enjoying this exhilarating aura of accepting our age difference, not letting that shit creep its deep dark toxin in to ruin these feelings.

"What are you going to get?"

He hugs me from behind and sways us as one unit.

"I'm thinking chocolate nut fudge brownie sounds amazing. You?"

"Such a hard choice, but I'm leaning towards strawberry cheesecake."

"Yum. We can both taste each other's."

"Oh definitely."

We place our order, scoop up our ice cream cups, and then settle into a corner high-top table. The ice cream shop is almost cold, but I guess that makes sense to keep the ice cream from melting too quickly.

I shiver. "Brrr. It's so chilly in here."

"I see your nipples," he says with a naughty grin.

"Good," I smirk. "They feel hard as buttons."

"Oh, trust me, they look more like thimbles, babe."

I chuckle and give him a sexy, sly grin. I love it when he says such things.

I feed him a spoonful of my ice cream. His eyes tell me he loves it.

"I really just want to eat that yum off your tits. We should have brought this back to the beach house to have some fun with it."

"Mm. I love how you think! And yes, please!" I clean off my spoon with my closed mouth, slowly prying it from my lips. "It likely would have melted too much with this heat. We'd need a cooler."

"True."

His expression turns contemplative.

"You ever honestly entertain the thought of moving here?"

I flick my eyes up to gaze into his. "Yeah. I actually have thought about it. Would be hard to be further away from Alex, and my sister and her family, and my mom and dad, but I think I'd actually love being a Floridian."

He smacks his lips and smiles. "It's settled then! When do you pack?" He claps his hands loudly.

I chuckle. "Slow down there, jockey. If I do it, it will take time. I'd have to sell my house at the minimum before I'd consider it." Oh, what am I getting myself into? I fill my cheeks with air, then let it blast out of my mouth. "Geez. Shit. Thinking of dealing with all the shit I've accumulated in my house and then go through it, then move it cross country is very overwhelming."

"I'd fly up and help. Every weekend until it's done." He looks so hopeful, I can't dash his fun thread of thoughts. "I'd do anything to get you down here. Can you imagine? We'd get to date like a normal couple."

I nod as the cold ice cream starts down my throat, making me even colder. "Oh, that's so cold," I mutter after I get the big spoonful down. I shudder, which makes my tits wiggle.

"Mmmm, please do that again. Pretty please," he says appreciatively. "Though my cock is filling my pants because of it."

I shimmy my shoulders and he sits back in his chair with a groan and a shift of his head to the left. "Fuck. Fuck me now," he mutters. After he recovers, he says, "But just think. You could go to the ocean anytime with your laptop and write. You'd be so inspired." He raises both hands in the air. "See! It would be so good for your work as well." His grin is huge, triumphant.

He's not wrong there. I raise my eyebrows at him as I swallow another spoonful of ice cream. "How can I argue with any of that?"

"We need anything for tonight's dinner, or are we set?"

"We are good. We've got the chicken breasts to grill, the spinach salad, multi-colored carrots, and rolls. Plus, we have two bottles of wine left, so we are good."

"Alright then. Let's get my car and head home."

The phrase sounds so nice, even if the idea is a bit of a pipe dream.

We hold hands as we walk out of the shop and dash through the hot humid air to the safety of the air conditioning in the car.

Chapter Twelve
Sebastian

I stir in bed, surprised I'm waking while it's still dark. My morning wood is adamant it's time to go fuck. I check my phone. The alarm is set to go off in twenty minutes for our final planned sunrise fucking session on the beach.

Wait. I hate that word. Final. Fuck that!

Memories of last evening intoxicate my slowly waking up brain and further harden my already hard as fuck cock. She was so happy, content, almost elated. It must be that she feels freer after admitting what she did. I watch her sleep, her chest rising and falling. She's so peaceful. And beautiful beyond any woman I've ever known. The notion of my feelings growing into something much deeper nudges at my heart once more. I dare myself to think it. I'm in love with her. I am. Dammit. I smile. It's a sheer joy to admit to myself. I resist the urge to touch her. I want to stroke her hair, her cheek, drag my fingers down her curvy body, savoring each rise and dip. My fingers twitch. I want to caress her so badly, but I'm going to let her sleep for twenty more minutes. Well, eighteen now. I click the alarm off. No way I'm falling back to sleep with this morning wood raging.

She shifts in her sleep to flat on her back, which makes her breast shift and nipple pop into view.

"I can't resist that beauty of a tit," I whisper as I lean over her bared breast.

I breathe over her nipple before I take it into my mouth. I wrap my lips around and suckle at her nipple.

She stirs against me as I have her pinned to the bed with my sucking. After a few seconds her eyes flutter open. "Mmmmm. Now there's a good way to wake up." Her voice is like soft butter even immediately upon waking.

Her hands dip into my hair. She strokes and tangles her fingers along my scalp, grabbing and tugging chunks of hair between her fingers.

I tug at her nipple with a hard suck, then lightly graze her hard nipple with my teeth.

"Oh fuck," she mutters as she writhes on the bed.

Her squirming is raging up my lust to max level. "We should just go outside now, before the sun rises."

She nods. "I have to pee first."

I reluctantly let her nipple fall free from my mouth. It plops out of me in a stiff peak and I want it back in my mouth pronto.

I sigh and let her squirm out of under me. I'd groan a complaint, but she's urgently making motions to get up.

We both head to the bathroom, both to pee, her first, and then we both brush our teeth, through matching devilish grins.

"This is going to be epic," I say. "I can't wait to love you under the sunrise."

She startles for a second but then seems all good. "Oh, me too. I really hope it isn't cloudy out so we can see it in its full glory." She grabs a big bath sheet from the cupboard. "Our fuck bed."

I pull her into my arms and she tucks her head into my chest. "Did I ever tell you I love the way your brain works?"

"Only about five hundred and one times, but I love to hear it again. And again. And again. And again."

I lean over so I can touch the tip of my nose to hers. "Let's go fuck." I take a step back and grab her hand.

She giggles as I pull her through the bedroom at a fast pace. We flat-out run through the darkened living room, making a beeline for the sliding door.

The air outside is beachy. I draw in a deep breath of salted air and sigh it back out. The roar of the waves makes it romantic without even trying. I tug her along down the stairs as the wind gently pampers us with its soft blow, intimate like its whisper to us. The scene couldn't be more perfect.

"Wow. It's amazing out here in the dark of the morning. Actually, it's a different feel than the dark of night," she mutters as we hit the sand.

"Yeah, I know exactly what you mean." Either it's because we've gotten sleep or because somehow the new day saturates us with itself, but it's refreshing and swollen with possibility.

Her breasts jiggle delicious and wild in her loose tank top as we trudge through the sand. God bless the inventor of sand to wade through. And God bless him for creating tits. And women. I don't think it's possible for her to turn me on more. I'm at peak desire for her. I stop and take the bath sheet from her. Together, we spread it across the rolling mounds of sand.

We reach for each other. Even in the dark, her eyes smolder. We crash our open mouths on each other. It's a debate whether our mouths or our hands are hungrier for each other. It's like I can't touch her enough. Okay. I lied. I can get more turned on.

She releases a little sigh-mewl which melts me.

"I want you, Ruan."

"I want you, Sebastian."

Our words rage up our passion higher and the wind cooperates with a sudden gust, which quickly dissipates back to a slow release of its breath. The dark sky shows no sign of sunrise yet. I wait with bated breath.

Our fondling of each other has exposed both her nipples. They call to me. I devour her right one in my mouth. Her perfect nipples on perfect breasts that could stop traffic or cause a car accident. I suckle her hard tit to the back of my throat as best as I can, which takes significant effort given how dense her breasts are. I fondle her other nipple, pinching it, tugging it, holding it like a cigarette as I squeeze my fingers together.

She responds with pleasured moans, her head falling back.

I grasp her back to steady her as my sucking causes her knees to buckle. I don't need her crashing to the ground like a sack of potatoes.

I release her nipple and drag my tongue over to her other one. I take it into my mouth and molest it properly, as such gorgeous nipples should be. I mouth worship her areola and massage her full nipple with my tongue before I do a full-on hard suck, hard as I can.

She groans out and the weight of her on my hand increases.

I swivel her to face the ocean and pull her back snug up to my front. My hard cock is a log between us. She reaches back to stroke it. I fondle her from behind paying attention to her breasts, her stomach, and hips, her pussy mound, relegating pussy touch for later in our foreplay to not only drive her crazier with want for my touch there, but also to heighten the sensuality of this fuck. I intend to fully make love to her in this fuck, more so than ever before. And she will come as much as I can muster.

Her right hand springs up and caresses my neck and hair. I sway us along with the motion of the ocean waves as I fondle and cradle her from behind. Her naked breasts swing as the straps of her tank top remain nestled snugly in her cleavage and on the right side of her right breast. Quite certainly the most seductive way to wear a tank top possible.

I play with her nipples as she undulates to my touch, moaning and mewling. Her sounds are delicious and arousing, raging my lust to want to pound her into submission. Her body squirming against mine is yummy, arousing every cell of me. But I take a deep breath to slow my lust down. I need to savor her. I won't get to taste her for way too long before we are together again. Not looking forward to that agonizing wait. When I'm forced to wait, it deepens the darkest pit in me. It's becoming surefire torture.

It's time for a bit of pussy touch. I sneak my hand into her pajama shorts and press her mound with my fingers. She responds with a happy humming sound.

"Mmmm. Yes."

I'm going to tease her, edge her desire up as high as I can before I fuck her. There's nothing more exquisite than a well-foreplayed woman who begs to be fucked.

I tickle my fingers along her vulva lips. They are moist and soft. A gentle dip in with my middle finger elicits a satisfied sound from her and my dominance swells a bit. I'm going to play her like the lovely fuck instrument she is, carry her into her sexual goddess state that will bring us mutual sexual bliss.

Her wetness increases as I press two fingers into her and oh so carefully pump them in and out of her. I speed it up, then rub the wet from her vagina across her swelling bean. She cries out in pleasure as I rub her clitoris in circles. I massage her clit, glazing her with her own internal juices. I drag my moist fingers up and over her mound to baste her skin before I slip my fingers back down into her cleft for her sweet spot.

She groans out and falls against me, weak. I go in for the kill and begin to slap her clit, spanking it with my hand. She completely comes undone. Her body starts to fall, so I cradle her harder with my arms and legs, curling my body into a C shape to support her full weight.

The sounds of her pussy are juicy as I slip two fingers in and continue to work her into a charged frenzy.

"Oh, fuck, Sebastian. I need you to fuck me. I need your cock in me. Please."

"Not yet, babe." I work my hands harder against the most intimate spots of her genitals. Her whimpers tell me she's getting so hot she is nearing the edge, so I pull back my efforts and remove my hand.

Her next sound is so cute. It sounds more like a pout than anything else. I swivel her to face me and take her face in my hands and full-on kiss her mouth. I slip my tongue into her to caress her tongue slowly with mine, then I show her my full hunger and really kiss her with full passion.

She releases hungry grunts and mine join hers as I slowly lay her down on the bath sheet while still kissing her. Once we are both on the blanket, I heavily pet her left breast and side down to her hips, reaching around to cup her ass cheek in my palm. I can easily palm her sweet apple buttock. I kiss down the side of her bottom, patiently waiting as I kiss every inch on my way down to reach her sweet round bottom. I open my mouth wide and press my teeth into her flesh. A slight bite that causes her to squeal and thrash. I grin with her ass cheek still between my teeth and heartily chuckle.

I lavish my tongue around her skin. The aroma of her pussy hits me full force as I straighten up. It's a musky scent she often gives off when it's been almost a full day since she has washed. It's a horny inducing smell that rages my dominance to the max. I push her body flat and spread her legs. This is all about my mouth pleasuring her, my hands teasing her to the edge, my passion igniting her before my cock will taste and dominate her lush pussy to first her orgasm, then mine. It's the only way.

I press my tongue along her slit to her happy moans. Her hands tangle in my hair, her fingers press my scalp, and her thighs cooperate by hard pressing my head. I want to eat her out so hard that her whole body curls around my head. I want her to fully encompass my head like she's smothering me. Like, I want to struggle to breathe, be that consumed by her desire and pleasure.

I tickle my tongue into her slit. She tastes salty and sweet, musky the way I'd love her to smell all the time.

I lean back and just breathe on her pussy. Her impatient whines make me smile.

"I just want to gaze upon your beautiful pussy for a few moments. You have such a gorgeous pussy, Ruan."

Her sounds turn from whines to appreciation. I chance a glance at her face and the happy smile there warms my heart and feeds my passion. I lick her like a lollipop for a few licks before I press my tongue into her vaginal opening. I fondle her with my tongue and then move on to rapidly tongue fucking her.

She moans and thrashes. I leave her insides alone as I travel my tongue up to molest her clit for a bit. Only the tip, then full licks, then full hard sucking of all her lady bits into my mouth. I press my fingers into her pussy and finger fuck her hard.

I want to say, 'I'm going to make you cum' but I'm too busy eating her out and I don't want to break her build to climax so I just keep on sucking her as she quickly escalates. Her body is thrashing and once she starts to twitch, then her body closes in on my head. I know she's raging into her climactic peak. Oh, the sweet body movements of success. Her sounds confirm she's coming as she moans and pants, screams out, then falls silent. Her pussy clamps down on my fingers and her vagina squeezes me. She gasps as it ramps down. Her moans turn to soft satisfied sighs.

I pull back from her groin. "Good girl to cum for me," I praise.

I lap at her pussy and eat all her juices that I fought hard to bring out.

"You're mine." I refuse to covet her, but love and claim, yes.

"I want to be yours," she parrots in her labored breathing.

I finish my meal of her and wipe my mouth with the back of my hand, hoping her juices will stain the scent of her into my skin. "You make a very yummy breakfast."

In my consumption of her pussy, I didn't notice the sunrise has started. The pinks and oranges have started to flood the sky. It's more a bath of emotion than just a mere sight.

"Did you see the sunrise start as I ate you out?" I ask, my voice full of hope.

"Yes. Oh, Sebastian, it was epic. Watching the sky erupt as I was exploding in my orgasm was so amazing. The likes I've never experienced before." Her eyes tell me the depth of what she has said.

This swells my ego, lame as that is, because this whole thing was what I wanted for her. I wanted to take her somewhere she's never gone before and I'm savoring that I succeeded in doing just that.

"You are utterly amazing," she whispers with a sleepy, happy expression.

I will keep that look in my heart forever, no matter what happens, I will never forget the look on her face. It's almost ... love.

"Wow. That was ...just wow!"

"I love wow." The teachings of an older lover taught me well when I was seventeen years old. The thoughts of Mandy Scolletti flood my brain. A sexy forty-one-year-old woman who changed me forever. She took my virginity but gave me the world. In her ministrations of sexual teaching, I got more from her than she got from me. I was a fumbling idiot, fixated on my cock. She taught me the pleasures of pleasuring a partner and gave me secrets to the mystery that was a female pussy that I could have never learned any other way. She was my sexual and sensual maestro. And to be honest, my piano teacher had not seduced me, I had seduced her. I learned so much from her that she set me on a trajectory that has landed me here with Ruan. A place I desire and value more than my own life. Ruan is becoming my life, as much as she has wanted to call us a fling, it's too late for that.

I settle in alongside her, hovering over her before I plant a deep French kiss. Her hand reaches for my cock in an instant. Her small hand is on my cock is perfection. The sunrise casts a glow of golden hue across her beautiful face. Her irises glow a brilliant bluish color in the sunrise's rays.

She props herself up on her elbows and then rises to her knees and bends down over my groin.

"I spy a bead of precum. I'm getting me a lucky drop." She sticks out her tongue above my swollen cockhead and then swipes her tongue across my slit.

I moan out. The touch of her soft, wet tongue sends a recoil across my body.

"Mmm," she mutters before doing it again. "Yummy. You are salty."

She consumes the whole head of my cock into her mouth and forms enough suction that my body floods with pleasure. She mouth humps my cock as her hand rides my shaft.

I groan out and my head falls back. Taking in the sight of the sunrise with her mouth wrapped around my cock sends me almost to my max threshold. My appreciation soaring. She is gifting me what I just gifted her. She sucks hard and her tits bounce.

I shudder. "Whoa, fuck. I'm gonna blow." I gently push her off, her mouth smacks as she pops her mouth off of me.

"So?" she says with a giggle.

"I want to max out. Come inside you."

"Mmmm. I want your cum inside me too."

We kiss again and I press her to lay back. I crawl between her legs as she spreads them to allow me space to fill in. My smile tells her I'm pleased as much as hers says take me.

I dangle my hard cock above her pussy, give it a few strokes, then present it to her lips. I lean in, which slips my cock barely into her, then I plunge in.

We both groan out. That first penetration always feels so fucking amazing. I slowly ride her, pumping my cock into her with thrusts that are hungry yet restrained. My lust wants me to pump fast, but my sensuality is getting me to slow fuck her.

She writhes beneath me, her hands roaming my upper body and reaching around to cup my ass. Her eyes fall closed and then reopen to meet my gaze as she appears to be enjoying the slow sex.

Remember to savor.

The waves continue to crash, blending their sounds into the air along with the cries of the birds. It's heaven. To be inside her, the sky sending its warm golden and pink hue across her creamy skin and blond hair, her eyes alight. I couldn't ask for any more than this moment to make my heaven real.

"Fuck me," she cries insistently. "I want you to fuck me hard."

I obey and begin to thrust into her more heartily. Her moans tell me she's riding up to her climax.

"Fuck me harder, Sebastian, please."

Oh, that delectable begging is sublime.

I please her with my cock. I use myself as a tool to play her, to play me, to lead us both up that orgasmic climb. As she approaches her peaking sounds, I command, "Come for me, Ruan. Come for me."

Her body reacts immediately into its contracting spasms as she twitches out another orgasm. I let loose and fuck her as hard as I want. She cries and screams and thrashes as she comes again, her fingernails digging into my flesh. I love when she falls into the rapid-fire mode of orgasming.

As her pussy clenches around my cock, I flood her hot insides with my warm cum. My grunts sound guttural as hers fall calmer. Her sighs and panting satisfy my ego. I've satisfied my woman. That's all I ever want. I'll come, and come again, but to satisfy her, that's the true satisfaction for me.

I kiss her on the lips and then lay beside her, spent. We both pant and watch as the sunrise blooms into full art right before our eyes. Skin on skin, post-sex on the beach, under the warm sunrise of a new morning, there's nothing better. It's a lesson in perfection I won't ever forget.

The ocean breeze caresses our naked bodies. Off in the distance, I see the first beach walkers coming our way. Well, at least the first to my knowledge. I pull her closer and drape the big bath sheet over her.

"Mm. I love snuggling with you after we fuck," she mutters dreamily.

I really want her to fall asleep on my shoulder, our bodies creamed together with comingled sweat and cum. I kiss her forehead as her eyes close.

#

Laying her down in our bed after the epic beach fuck had been a treat. Pleasuring her with my body and sex toys to twenty-five more orgasms had been the ultimate treat. But laying here with her asleep, fully satisfied, is the best treat that tops them all. I watch her breathe as she slumbers. Traces of satisfaction and happiness are still somehow blissfully settled on her face as she is unconscious. What a gift. If only I could wake up this way every morning. I'd be so happy. The wistful smile on my face does not wane, only grows as I dwell on every second with her, even as she is asleep.

After an hour and a half, I nudge her awake. I kiss her forehead as she squirms, her eyelids all aflutter.

"Babe, we've got to start making preparations for you to go." It hurts to say it.

Her lip puffs out in a pout.

I kiss it.

"I know. It totally sucks."

Her eyes take on a look of desperation, which she quickly shuts down. She glances at the clock. "Yeah. I guess you're right. I don't want to have to buy another plane ticket because I miss my flight."

"Ok. You shower. I'm going to scrounge up some breakfast for us."

She nods with a yawn, and a stretch of her arms, then torso. She looks so sexy, I'd give anything to fuck her again, but there isn't time.

"That was so epic, by the way. The whole morning, mind-blowing. Positively the best ever."

"Yes, it really was. I will keep it forever in my thoughts, never forget it no matter what."

She gets an odd look on her face, which then falls somber. "Right. Me neither."

I decide to let it go and not ruin this moment. She likely just doesn't want to leave and is struggling with admitting it to herself.

"Thank you," she says before disappearing into the bathroom. "You take such good care of me."

"I'd do a full day just about you today."

Her smile is sweet, genuine, and her eyes tell me that comment struck a chord.

I slip on some boxers and head to the kitchen to see what breakfast foods we have left. The rest of the food she told me to take home. No sense in throwing out good food. And I'll certainly eat it, no doubt. I'm a damn glutton.

I set out the last three croissants, some strawberries, cream cheese, and the last slivers of steak warmed up. I brew the coffee. Just as I sit down to enjoy my first cup of brew, she emerges looking all fresh and new, just absolutely stunning in a white sleeveless button-up top showing off her generous cleavage, and a hot pink skirt that shows how scrumptious her hips curve into her thighs.

"Wow. You look gorgeous. You are glowing."

"It's all the sex. No. It's all the orgasms." She grins as she takes a seat next to me. Her eyes are so bright and brilliant.

I pop up and grab a mug for her for coffee. "We have just enough creamer left for you to have it how you like it."

I fix up the coffee for her as she smiles at me, touches my back. Her head falls to my shoulder and all I want to do is pull her into my arms. So, I do.

She sighs happily.

"I'm feeling very sappy," I confess.

"Me too. Like a mountain strangling me."

I laugh. "Well, that doesn't sound very pleasant!"

I lean back and snatch her chin in my fingers.

My heart dives. Tears are welling up in her beautiful eyes.

"Oh, Sebastian. I just …"

I pull her to me immediately. "Oh, babe. Me too."

I hold her tight, hoping she won't sob. I don't want that to be in our last minutes together. She seems to calm before she pulls away from me.

She laughs and it's like I've stepped back into the sun.

"I just had the most amazing week. I don't want it to end yet."

I can't resist another prompt. "So, maybe that's a sign to move here." I bite my lower lip and let my eyes ring hopeful.

She smirks. "I think planning our next getaway will help me. I'll start researching on the plane."

My heart swells to hear this and if we have to take baby steps, it's better than a wall.

"Yes. I'll make it happen whenever you book it for. I can help look if you'd like."

She nods. "Yeah, I guess two looking is better than one."

We enjoy our breakfast out on the deck under the warm sun, chatting to the ever-constant sound of the waves.

Her phone rings. She stares at it and hesitates, but then answers it.

"Hi sweetie, how are you?"

Her face falls into a myriad of emotions, from skeptical, to slightly angry, to frustrated as she listens.

"Alex. You don't need to worry. I know what I'm doing." Though she says this, her face says otherwise.

A black rot erupts in my gut. I had never considered her son being a part of her roadblock to accepting us.

"Alex, I have to go. My flight is soon. We need to leave for the airport."

She nods.

Dread fills me further as her face clouds more.

"Yes. I will. Love you, bye."

"All okay?" I ask immediately.

She glances at me but doesn't hold my gaze. "Yeah, yeah. That was just Alex."

"Not a happy feel-good call, I see." I reach for her hand and pet the top of it.

"He's just worried about me is all."

"Worried about you, with me, right?"

She nods slowly and finally holds her eyes to mine. "He's just worried. It's nothing."

Geez. We don't need more than her trepidation casting doubt, let alone her son's.

I don't want to know the answer to the question that's filling me with fear, but if I don't ask it, it'll eat at me until I do. I hold my breath, then release it before I ask, "Does he not accept you with me?"

She shakes her head and I feel all the progress we've reached this week drain away.

"But he will be fine with it. And really, I don't care. It's my life, not his."

So, there is more to it than just her own doubts. Well, fuck.

"It's not a matter for us to think about in our last minutes together."

I almost believe her.

"I'm so happy we got your car back before I am leaving." She smiles and it's an effort.

"Yeah, me too." I glance at my phone. "It's time. We'd better head out in case we hit traffic. I'm really glad we already returned the rental."

She nods and rises. She peers out across the ocean and blows it a kiss. "Til next time, beautiful friend."

It feels like an ending, and I hate it.

We tidy up the kitchen while not talking, which is unlike us, and I hate it.

She pauses while packing up the food in a bag. "I shouldn't have answered the phone in our last minutes together. I just wanted to hear his voice before I got on the plane and he's so busy, I always try to answer when he calls. I don't like flying. The fear of death always plagues me." She almost looks scared. "I wanted to hear his voice again, just in case."

"Oh, shit. Don't even talk that way! Flying is safer than driving."

"I know it's irrational, but I always feel that way. I can't wait to get off the plane, to be honest."

"It will be okay, babe." I give her a hug and stroke her hair. I didn't anticipate all this.

"I just wish I hadn't answered it. I don't want this to get you down. And just when I'm just getting to a good place."

"We are in a good place. Nothing can change that."

She nods, but her eyes tell me otherwise.

How can I convince a man I've never met that I have good intentions about a woman we both love?

We start to load my car and before long we are on the road. It's a painful drive with way too much silence, but at least we're holding hands. I squeeze her hand and glance her way every so often. Eventually, her eyes look happier, her smile grows more relaxed. I wish I had a few more hours to get her feeling good again.

"I had a wonderful time this week with you. I really can't say that enough." She fidgets in her seat. "We really stretched our sexual relationship too."

"Oh, did we ever! I'm actually a bit shocked still that I fucked a dude's butt! I may never get over that!"

She bursts out laughing and it's what we needed.

"Never thought I'd pack a dude's fudge."

She gasps then laughs harder, her hand covers her mouth.

When her laughter dies down, she says, "I never thought I'd be a good little kitten either. Well, I wasn't that good. I was a bit uncooperative."

"You did great! I was happy. You came. I came. What else do we need?"

"True. But you know, I realized we kind of fucked up. Remember we had a plan for the edible chocolate body paint? I failed because I didn't even remember to pack it."

"Next time! I'm hungry for it already. We need beat the expiration date, so there's another reason to get together sooner rather than later. We can't waste that!"

"True. Whew. That's making me hot to think about," she says as she wiggles her butt in the seat.

"Ditto," I say as that first surge of blood bolts into my cock. "My cock agrees."

She immediately reaches to fondle my groin.

We match our smiles.

"Too bad we are at the airport, or I'd give you road head again."

"Dang, if only we had more time, I'd drive around more just so you could." We literally don't have time.

"Maybe I can try." Her little smile is so sexy and seductive, I can't disagree, even though we are literally pulling into the airport.

She unzips my shorts and pulls my cock out. She's at me like an anaconda, sucking and stroking so fast. She slips out a tit and that's all it takes. I come hard in her mouth as I'm slamming on the brakes.

"Uh, fuck! Fuck fuck!" I mutter as my cock spasms emptying into her mouth.

She rights herself in the seat with a giant grin, as if she had never left her seat. Her sweet innocent face would convince everyone of it too. "Thanks for cooperating by being quick. We needed a flash flood."

"Mm. Wow. That was damn good and yeah, a little too quick!"

"It was perfect."

I park the car at the drop-off zone. My body is shaking a bit after that fast blow job, but I get out of the car like a jackrabbit.

I pull out her suitcase and carry-on bag, set the suitcase on its wheels, and hand her the laptop bag.

"Gonna write on the flight?" I ask, admiring her answer before she answers.

"Yep, I'm itching to use some of our experiences in stories so I'm going to write them out while they are fresh." She pauses, her hand on the suitcase handle. "You sure you don't mind if I use some of what we do in books?"

"Oh, damn, Ruan. I absolutely love that you do."

"I really love how it immortalizes us. As if we are really legit."

"Yes. I love that more than you can know."

"Good. Me too."

We embrace. The strong grip she uses to hug me astonishes me. The look of fear crosses her eyes again and I want to smash it away.

"You will be safe, babe. And we will be together again very soon." I wish more than anything I could fly with her, hold her hand and make her feel safer by my presence.

"I know."

Her hesitancy is either about us, Alex, or the flight, and I'm only hoping one is the main cause.

I almost say it.

"Thank you," she says, interrupting my fear, which saves me from not saying what I really want to say.

"Thank you." I'm settled. I don't want this sad moment to be the time I say it to her. Besides, why put her on the spot when she already has reservations.

I reluctantly let go of her as she steps back.

"I'll call you when I land."

"Please do."

After a last longing glance, she turns and walks out of my sight, which feels way too much like out of my heart for my comfort.

To be continued in the next getaway trip...

Did you catch Ruan and Sebastian's first getaway to the Colorado mountainside, where sex was their focus more than their hearts? Check it out on online sellers. Get all the smutty sexy and intense fun of Ruan and Sebastian's first getaway fling in: **Ruan's Cabin Getaway**.

About the Author

Ruan Willow is an erotica author, a sexuality/sexual health and wellness podcaster at Oh F*ck Yeah with Ruan Willow (free on podcast apps and on Full Swap Radio, an internet radio station and app), and an erotic NSFW audiobook narrator. She is also published on Literotica and Frolic Me online, as well as other sites. She loves interacting with fans, cooking, sex, reading, sex, being outdoors, spending time with family and friends, travel, swimming, sex, podcasting, and more sex. Did you catch all the sex? She's giggling right now thinking about you reading all about sex. Yup, she loves to laugh!

Thank you for purchasing this book! Pink Infinity Publishing LLC and Ruan Willow thank you!

Letter from Ruan:

Thank you so much for reading my book! I happily wrote book one in this series, Ruan's Cabin Getaway, in response to a fan's request. This current book, Ruan's Beach Getaway, grew from the story of Ruan and Sebastian that blossomed in my mind through time. They had to continue their story, their journey of love, sex, and exploration, so it flowed through me.

My fans are my main focus, but of course, I want to like what I write too, and I thoroughly enjoyed writing this story. I am where I am because fans responded to me and my writing, and my podcast, so I owe everything to all of you! You are a blessing in my life, and you give me more joy than you will ever know. I love interacting with fans and I will never ever give that up. Please connect with me on social media!

This book is an erotic romance, heavy on the sex because that's what my fans love and I'm happy to oblige. I hope you read the other books in this series as well, there will be at least one more.

If you'd like to experience more of my work, here is the website for my sexuality/erotica podcast, my books, my website, my Patreon, my social media, and all my links:

https://linktr.ee/RuanWillow

Thank you for purchasing this book. *I'd love to hear your thoughts in an honest review on the site where you purchased the book from.* It warms my heart profusely when I see someone has taken the time to review my book. Love you all very much!

I want to thank all my family and friends for all of their support. I'd be lost without you.

More from Ruan:

Want Ruan to narrate your book? She has an account on ACX. Send her a message on ACX to get in contact with her.

All Ruan's Links in one spot: https://linktr.ee/RuanWillow

Oh Fck Yeah with Ruan Willow Podcast:

https://ohfckyeahwithruanwillow.buzzsprout.com/

Her website is https://ruanwillowauthor.com/

You can sign up on her website to be on her email list to be notified of updates.

Ruan's other books:

Ruan's Getaway Series:
Ruan's Cabin Getaway, Book 1
Ruan's Beach Getaway, Book 2
Magic In Her Kisses
The Sex Challenge Series:
The Kitchen Sex Challenge Book 1
The Grocery Store Sex Challenge Book 2
Inside of Ruan Willow
The Mardi Gras Unmasking
Ruan is in the following anthologies:
He Will Obey
The Femdom Coven

Don't miss out!

Visit the website below and you can sign up to receive emails whenever Ruan Willow publishes a new book. There's no charge and no obligation.

https://books2read.com/r/B-A-TOPT-VZJYB

BOOKS 2 READ

Connecting independent readers to independent writers.

Did you love *Ruan's Beach Getaway*? Then you should read *Ruan's Cabin Getaway*[1] by Ruan Willow!

Dive right into their affair in Book1! Strangers to lovers, MILF Ruan and younger man Sebastian meet on an online dating app and begin to date long-distance. After a history of hours of Facetime, texting, sexting, and phone calls, they decide to meet in person for a romantic weekend. Despite their age gap difference, Sebastian and Ruan desperately want to spend time together. A rustic cabin in the mountains is the first choice in their plan.They engage in explicit steamy and passionate sex in every room of the cabin, including the pool and hot tub, office, and kitchen. They can't get enough of each other, nor enough of the age play, light experimental BDSM, and good heart-filled romance they indulge in. With goals of fulfilling each

---

1. https://books2read.com/u/medqrV

2. https://books2read.com/u/medqrV

other's fantasies, they find themselves craving more weekend meetups in the future. Even though life is busy with Ruan as an author and Sebastian working hard at his job, the cabin getaway weekend blossoms with the promises of more sensual adventures to come.Please note this spicy book is heavy with sex scenes. If you like a lot of hot sexual activity in your books, this book is for you!

Read more at https://ruanwillowauthor.com/.